CURSED

THE CURSE TRILOGY BOOK 1

NICOLE MARSH

CASSY JAMES

MIRABELLA LOVE

I was a normal, reclusive girl, dealing with the typical stuff. Like getting bullied by my hot, but rude ex-best friend and navigating my first job.

Around my birthday things in my town become... strange. My mom pulls me aside and reveals a shocking family legacy. The confession creates a snow-ball effect, and things get even weirder.

Suddenly, I go from being a normalish girl to being a girl with untapped magic, three potential love inter-ests, a secret grandma, and a council of werewolves breathing down my neck. All while scrambling to learn more about a centuries old curse that no one seems very concerned about.

What could possibly go wrong?

CONTENTS

PROLOGUE

Mirabella

Thirteen Years Ago

Pushing open my bedroom door, I climb down the steep stairs toward the living room, dragging my bunny behind me to watch for monsters. A quick peek around the corner reveals my parents nestled together on the couch. The floorboards creak as I shift my weight, immediately catching my mom's attention.

She hears everything.

Both pairs of eyes in the room, one blue and one gray, turn to face me. "Mira, why aren't you in bed?" My mom asks.

"I couldn't sleep," I whisper, squeezing my stuffed bunny closer to my body.

"It's very late, you need to rest before school tomorrow, kiddo," my dad replies.

Together they move as a unit, rising from the couch and approaching me at the edge of the room. My dad swoops me into his arms easily, carrying me up the stairs as my mom trails behind us.

My dad gently places me on my bed, tucking the blanket around my body, then sits at the end near my feet. My mom perches near my head, running her fingers through my hair, her nails lightly scraping my scalp.

"Will you tell me a story?" I ask quietly.

"Which one?" My mom replies as she settles against the bed frame next to me, tucking a strand of her blonde hair behind her ear as she lounges backwards.

"The fairytale about our town," I reply, already feeling sleepier from the warmth of my bed and the soothing rhythm of my mother's fingers playing with my hair.

"Okay. The legend of our town starts..."

Unsettled Territory in the Northwestern United States
Almost Two-Hundred Years Ago

THE CARRIAGE WHEELS roll to a stop on a patch of lush grass just past the edge of a densely wooded area. The clearing stretches for over a mile, the edge of a cliff leading to the ocean just visible in the distance. A family of four disembarks from its tight quarters, stretching tired muscles after the lengthy ride lasting almost a dozen days.

"Is this the spot?" A young boy asks his parents, taking in the empty expanse of land. "I can see the water! Is this the place?"

"Yes, son," His father says with a laugh, ruffling his dark hair gently. "We will settle this land and name it after our family." As the words leave his lips, another carriage rolls into the green pasture, the wheels slowly stopping as the horses whinny.

This carriage is ornate, more than necessary for traveling into the unsettled western lands. A man hops off the box and steps towards the family of four. "Hello there, neighbors. I see you've found our plot of land," his gravelly voice bellows.

Alerted by the noise, two women peek their head out the carriage door to check on the scene. Spotting their faces, a second man jumps down from the box and opens the door, assisting them down the step. Two light-haired women that appear to be sisters emerge, one of them pregnant and holding a toddler. Another man disembarks from the trailer behind them.

"Your land?" The father from the family of four asks. "We were the first to arrive here, there are no signs that this land has been settled."

"We have been staying in town, gathering supplies to build our home," a man from the ornate carriage states in his gruff voice.

"How can we be certain you did not follow us? That

this is not a lie?" The father from the family of four asks.

Another man from the ornate carriage steps forward with tense muscles. "You accuse us of lying?"

Before things can escalate further, the blond toting her toddler steps in his path. She tugs him to the side, whispering fervently in his ear. The family on the other side is curious what she is saying, but the distance is too far to hear her words.

When the pair finally separate, the man looks more relaxed. He speaks again. "My wife has proposed a solution, to settle this dispute. We see the babe you are holding is a little girl. We would like to join our families, when the time comes, by marrying her to our son."

Present Day

"TELL ME ABOUT THE WEDDING," I interrupt before a long yawn.

My mom laughs, scraping her hand through my hair again. "So impatient," she teases, but obliges in my request.

"Years pass and the two families are to be joined by marriage..."

Florence, OR
One-Hundred and Eighty-Five Years Ago

"I DON'T UNDERSTAND why I have to marry that vulgar man. He spends most of his time in the woods. He's basically half savage," Isobel whines. She stands in front of the glass in her parents' home, her mother behind her lacing the strings of a corset, tightly yanking the contraption to give her daughter the perfect hourglass figure.

Her mother laughs in response, continuing to seal her daughter into her wedding dress. "His family owns a lumber mill; he has to be near the trees to mill the wood."

There is less than an hour remaining before she's set to march down the aisle and into a marriage she doesn't want. Despite her previous protests being ignored and guests already arriving at the church, Isobel continues her plight. "Yes, but we discovered GOLD. Our family is a class above his and this marriage no longer makes sense," she argues.

"We gave our word, many years ago. You will honor our family and marry Arthur," her mother admonishes.

Isobel huffs, but is smart enough to know when she's lost an argument to her mother. She sulks in front of the mirror, admiring the flowing white dress her mother is buttoning up her back. At least she will look like a queen during the ceremony.

Suddenly, the door to the room flies open and a man bursts in. Both women shriek until they realize it's Isobel's father.

"Father, what are you doing here?"

"It's Arthur," He wheezes out. "He's left town with the general store's daughter."

Isobel's jaw unhinges and her mother freezes, eyes wide. "What does this mean?" She asks.

"It means the wedding is off."

Present Day

"AND THEN THEY GET CURSED, RIGHT?" I ask, barely able to keep my groggy eyes open.

My mom laughs, "I've told you this story too many times. Next time, you'll have to tell me." She leans forward, brushing my hair away from my forehead and placing a soft kiss. "But yes, a curse was placed on the family that broke their promise."

"The magic was too strong though right," I prod, wanting her to continue.

"You're right, the magic was too strong and it affected both families. The magic continued to grow and affect the entire town, causing it to divide right down the middle. Everyone who comes to Florence now has to choose a side."

"How can the curse go away?"

"Legend says it can only be cured if the eldest from each family line marry."

"Is the curse real, mommy?" I ask, but like always, before I hear her reply, I'm fast asleep.

1

THE DINNER

Mirabella

A faint, misty rain drifts down from above, lightly coating my hair and skin. Ignoring the moisture, I rest my hip against the cool, metal rail of the balcony attached to my room. It's always been one of my favorite places, with its two contrasting views.

Leaning over the middle of the rail, I'm able to see a cliff overhanging the water on my left, with waves crashing against the rocky side. To my right is a view of sloping houses backed by massive trees, with small woodland creatures occasionally darting into the open.

My entire life I've been admiring these views, it's one of the best things about my home.

I live in an insignificant town, Florence, on the Northwestern coast of the states. Like the majority of the North West, the weather is mostly soggy year-round and lush green forests surround the town. Overall, Florence is nice, a small, sleepy place with a population of about six thousand people.

Nothing much ever happens here.

Soon the most exciting part of the year will arrive; we'll experience our annual tourist season. A number of people visit our town during the summer months, to admire our one claim to fame, an operational lighthouse that's a century old. Natives often refer to these visitors as the kooky lighthouse fanatics, as they tend to be obsessed. Spending their summer months exploring as many as they can and buying up all the lighthouse related paraphernalia available in town, including the cheesy magnets sold downtown.

The only other thing of interest about Florence is the tale of the conflict that caused our town to become divided.

The Main Road in town acts as a bit of a line between the wealthier houses lining the coast and the more modest homes near the woods. Money doesn't seem to be the reason behind the divide, just a notable difference between the two sides of town.

Over the years, each side has developed their own schools through grade twelve and separate grocery stores. There's still some common ground in the downtown area, but if you're from one side of town, you rarely mingle with the other side intentionally.

Most newcomers purchase their residence and follow tradition—avoid mingling and never leave. It's just the way things have been, for as long as anyone can remember.

If you believe local legend, the town was split down the middle shortly after it was settled, due to a disagreement between the founding families. The feud led to a curse being placed on both sides and the divide will remain until it's broken. Of course, it's unlikely that Florence is being affected by a centuries old magic spell, but small towns sure love their gossip.

"Mira! Come downstairs to greet the Morts!" My mom yells up the stairs, interrupting my thoughts.

Releasing a deep sigh, I tear my gaze from the slice of town visible from my balcony and step back inside. I've reached the point of maximum avoidance. Resigned, I face my bedroom, my eyes sweeping over my pale pink walls, sturdy gray canopy bed, and my small, pale gray sofa. My assessment of the room ends at my vanity with its attached mirror, then my eyes flit to my door.

I wish that I could just curl up on my bed or go to my studio and paint. But I know my parents would never allow me to skip their beloved weekly tradition.

Walking to my mirror, I conduct one last check before heading downstairs. I'm wearing a new, white sundress that my mom left hanging on the back of my door this morning. It has dark, wooden buttons down the front. The bust is tight, but the dress flares out down around my hips, ending near my ankles. It's the perfect length for my petite frame. My waist length blonde hair is flowing down my back in loose curls, completing 'the look'.

Earlier, my mom came upstairs to see me in the dress. She fawned over me, telling me how beautiful and grown up I look. I'm "her beautiful young woman!" now. I never wear much makeup, but she added some mascara and winged eyeliner to "make my gray eyes pop", and a little dark pink lipstick to "make my lips poutier".

My reflection mimics my movements as I turn my head side to side, regarding my heart-shaped face in the mirror. The image shows my almond eyes look larger and my lips look fuller. My mom applies makeup like a professional, never failing to dress up my looks when I allow it.

Dragging my eyes from the mirror, I hurry towards the door, attempting to avoid the inevitable ire that will ensue, if my mom has to call me again. I trudge down the stairs like it's a death sentence instead of a dinner with my parents' best friends and their son.

With a deep inhale, I square my shoulders and round the last corner to the sitting room. The door is open, and I pause again, allowing the quiet conversation to wash over me before I step foot inside.

Sunday dinner is the highlight of my parent's week. I wish the feeling was mutual, but by four o'clock on Saturday, every week, my belly fills with a solid ball of dread, already wishing it was Monday.

The Morts are nice enough, except for their son Vlad. He's a monster.

"Mirabella, you become more stunning every time I see you!" Vlad's mother, Tricia, exclaims, swarming me as soon as I step foot into the room. Her curtain of dark hair swishes with her movements as she stoops down to wrap me in a warm hug, while gushing over my dress. "Where is this from? You look beautiful in white!"

I murmur, "Thank you." The words barely audible as I'm still wrapped in her tight hold, my cheeks smooshed against her chest from the grip. With one final pat, she releases me.

As soon as she steps away, my gaze sweeps over the room. I notice Mr. Mort, or Bart as he insists I call him, next. We exchange a small wave before my eyes flit to my parents, standing wrapped around each other with joyful grins.

With morbid curiosity similar to watching a car crash, my eyes continue to scan the room, despite knowing the next person they will find. My eyes land on Vlad, lounging on one of the couches. I fight the irritation over the fact that he's here. Neither of us have a choice in the matter.

Vlad is incredibly handsome, tall with the musculature of a roman deity. He has a sculpted face and thick, black hair that he wears short on the sides, with a longer portion on the top. It's always swept back off his forehead in a dramatic fashion like he just walked out of a tornado and simply pushed the strands out of his face afterwards. Yet, somehow, the style makes him appear sexy instead of sloppy.

I know from experience, though, his exterior is his only attractive feature.

His amber gaze collides with mine and his neutral expression transforms into a deep, furious scowl. Vlad always reacts this way, but it still stings. My eyes continue to drink in his movements as he turns to his side, and that's when I notice he's brought a friend.

On Vlad's left sits Marvin, one of his buddies from High School. The pair were co-captains of the football team and have remained close ever since. Like Vlad, Marvin is also tall and broad shouldered, but with lighter brown hair and coffee-colored eyes. Unlike Vlad, he isn't a vindictive jerk. My honest opinion of Marvin is that he's a big, dumb jock that probably peaked in High School.

As if he can feel my eyes on him, Marvin glances up from his conversation and our eyes immediately lock. I waffle over waving hello as his assessing gaze sweeps over my body. When his eyes return to my face, his expression isn't hostile like Vlad's but I also wouldn't consider it welcoming.

My family's butler, Jacob, enters the room, saving me from deciding. "Dinner is served, if you would please follow me," he announces.

In a slight shuffle, I join the single file line entering the dining room. Somehow, during the chaos, I end up between Marvin and Vlad. As we filter to the seats surrounding the table, the order of the line sticks and I unintentionally become seated between the pair.

As my butt hits the cushioned seat, I release a sigh

and send up a small prayer. I repeat my request that Vlad allows me to eat in peace for the next hour, twice, just in case anyone's listening.

Across the table, Mr. Mort's eyes focus on Vlad and I. To say he looks elated at our seating arrangement would be an understatement. My mother is also hiding a small, secretive smile behind her wineglass, as her eyes glance at the small space left between us.

I exhale another sigh, already knowing both our parents will spend at least half the night talking about this. They're delusional and think Vlad and I are still best friends, like we used to be years ago. They hope someday we'll end up married, joining our two families so they can be related.

Just a case of people wanting to see what they want, I guess.

"What are your plans for your last summer after high school?" Tricia asks me, after Jacob serves the first course.

Darting a brief glance at my parents, I respond, "I was thinking about applying to be a part-time assistant at the library."

I hear my mom's sharp inhale, but avoid eye contact. My gaze focuses on the caesar salad in front of me. I stab at the lettuce gathering as many leaves onto the fork as possible, as if I plan to take a very large bite. Really, it's just a stall tactic.

My mom's sharp inhale is essentially meritless, anyway. Technically, the library is on the opposite side of the Main Road, but people from both sides check out books. I'm uncertain she's reacting to the location, but it's either that or the fact I sprung this plan on them without prior discussion.

I don't really need the money, but Sylvia, my one and only friend in Florence, was recently accepted as a future "hair designer". The school is just outside of town and her classes start two weeks after we graduate.

I'm taking a few art classes at the community college in the fall, but there's a few months before those begin. Instead of moping around the house all summer, I thought I could work at the library, earning cash and gaining experience.

"Oh, dear, you don't want to work at the library! It's so stuffy and boring." Tricia exclaims. She looks pensive for a minute, tapping her long, red nails on the tablecloth while her brain processes data. "I know! Vlad has been working at the *F.O. Daily*. He could probably get you an intern position. Then you two could spend your summer together, like you used to!"

The *F.O. Daily,* also referred to as The Daily, is our town's local newspaper. Nothing really exciting happens in our town, so it's mostly fluff pieces, marriage announcements, and business ads, with the occasional hard hitting piece or expose.

One time we had a homeless person who wandered through our town. Literally wandered through. He was here for about three hours before he moved on to greener pastures. That homeless man was front page news for three weeks until the local pie baking competition finally replaced his story.

Despite the lack of exciting news, the paper is popular in Florence and almost everyone subscribes.

I glance up from my plate, where I've begun mashing all my food together with my fork. My eyes scan the table, taking in everyone's expressions.

My mom and Tricia both appear ecstatic over the prospect of Vlad and I spending summer together. My dad and Bart are both holding up glasses of whisky and talking in quiet voices on the other end of the table, not making their feelings known about the matter. I chance a peek next to me and Vlad has adopted a pained expression, which doesn't surprise me. I don't bother examining Marvin. The entire dinner he's been shoveling food in his mouth and I doubt he's even paying attention.

I open my mouth to respond, intending to give a vague 'I'll think about it', when suddenly a splash of cold liquid lands in my lap. Glancing down, I find a brown stain quickly spreading across the white fabric covering my thighs. Scanning the area near me, my eyes almost immediately spot Vlad's smirking face. His hand is holding an empty glass just past the edge of the table, still turned to the side.

Typical Vlad.

Within seconds, the liquid has seeped through the fabric of my dress and I jump from my seat at the shock to my skin. Some soda sprays onto the white tablecloth and my entrée. "What the heck, Vlad?" I demand, my words spiked with loathing.

Vlad attempts to flatten his lips from a smirk into

something more contrite. "Sorry Little Mir, it slipped." He says, his tone innocent even as he struggles to keep a full-blown grin off his face.

"Oh, Mira. What an unfortunate accident," My mom chimes in, appearing sorrowful over the current state of my dress.

Tricia agrees, "What a shame for that beautiful piece."

Looking down, I see the pristine white cloth is stained and probably beyond repair. I force my lips to remain sealed, when all I want to do is scream accusations at Vlad and force him to apologize.

Fighting my urges, I excuse myself from the table, "I need to go change. I'll be right back."

Back in my room, I rip the dress over my head and throw it into the hamper. Hopefully, the stain will come out, since it was brand new and pretty.

Well, before Vlad destroyed it. I huff over his childish actions, annoyed all over again. I allow myself to be angry another minute before brushing the thought aside to address my current clothing situation.

As I stride to my closet, I call Sylvia to tell her about the soda fiasco. Sylvia is the only person who has been willing to ignore the wild rumors spread by Vlad and his cronies and become my friend. Her family moved here during the ninth grade and they're all rebels.

They live on our side of town, but they mingle with everyone. Her parents also caused a scandal when they first arrived, refusing to be featured on the front page

THE RIDE

Mirabella

G raduation Day.

I've been dreaming of this since high school began. Some of those dreams admittedly turned into nightmares. Ones where I forgot to wear a dress under my graduation gown, or throwing my cap into the air takes out someone's eye. But I'm trying to push past those fears and appreciate no longer having to spend eight hours a day trapped in a brick building, suffering the verbal and physical abuse of my classmates.

This past week school has been extra hellacious, as students packed in last-minute pranks while they still could. Being the first to leave every class and bolting straight to my car at the last bell, still didn't keep me unscathed from my bullies.

It doesn't matter though, now that's all just a part of

almost ten minutes and I don't want my mom to come looking for me.

When I return to the table, Vlad shoots me another smirk, coughing behind his hand to cover a laugh. His rudeness sparks something inside of me. Rage bubbles to the surface of my skin and I react, which is out of character for me, but I'm fed up.

Instead of sitting, I stand behind my chair and clear my throat loudly. I wait for everyone to cease talking and give me their full attention before I make my grand announcement. "I thought about it while I was upstairs. I would love to intern at *F.O. Daily*. What comes next?"

at his JOB. You have the chance to make him look bad in front of the entire town, which would be pretty sweet revenge if you ask me."

Now I'm the one hmming. While I contemplate her words, I snag a short-sleeved, blush pink dress off a hanger and slip it over my head. "I guess. But what if something goes wrong?" I eventually ask, as the fabric is clearing my head and sliding down my body. The phone is still tucked between my ear and my shoulder and the weird angle of my arm causes the dress to catch. I almost miss Sylvia's next words as I hop around and wiggle, attempting to coax the dress the rest of the way on.

"It's at his workplace though," She insists. "He won't be able to get away with everything he does at your house or through his cronies at school."

Her words make sense, but I have a gut feeling Vlad would still find a way to torment me, he's creative like that. After a few minutes of thinking it over, I finally reply, "I'm not so sure, but I'll at least consider your suggestion."

My words pacify Sylvia, and she makes a noise of approval in the back of her throat. "I have so many ideas for revenge that you could use at work." Her tone is pure evil and I expect her to blurt out a 'mwahaha' next, but somehow, she restrains herself.

"I haven't made any decisions yet," I remind her, then quickly end the call before she spews her extensive list of revenge ideas. "Hey, I need to get back to dinner. I'll text you after." I've already been gone of *F.O. Daily* as newcomers, which was previously unheard of.

Using my shoulder to hold my phone to my ear, I flip through my hangers. I'm searching for something that my mom would deem appropriate for dinner with guests. As I look, a part of me wishes I brought her upstairs to dress me.

Sylvia answers the phone on the first ring. "Thought it was time for your weekly dinner with Vlad the asshole." She states drolly into the receiver. In the brief pause following her statement, I can hear her two brothers shouting about the TV in the background, so I'm guessing she got stuck babysitting.

"It is," I confirm. "He just threw his drink all over me." She releases a low growl at my words, but I continue, "His mom thinks I should intern at *F.O. Daily*, so we can spend the summer together."

This time, Sylvia emits a hmming noise, indicating that she's mulling something over. From experience, I know it's not worth it to say another word until she's done thinking and has checked back into the conversation.

"You should do it, become the intern," she says, following her hmm of thought.

"Uhm, what?" I ask, almost dropping my phone from shock. That's the conclusion she's come to? Many magnificent ideas have come from Sylvia's hmms, but this is definitely not one of them.

"Come on Mira," she starts. "He's tortured you for YEARS, and now you have a chance to mess with him my past. Today is the end of an era. No more "Queer Mir" or "Mira UNLoveABLE" being painted onto my locker. No more rotten meat stuffed into my backpack.

Today it all ends.

I stroll into the kitchen with extra pep in my step. Nothing will get me down, today will be a great day. A new beginning, if you will. I'm humming, traipsing straight to the fridge to grab orange juice and bolstering myself with happy thoughts when a flash of something black catches the corner of my eye. My head whips into a double take and my feet stop of their own volition at the sight of a broad shouldered, dark-haired form sitting on the bench in our kitchen.

I close my eyes.

No. Freaking. Way.

That better not be Vlad in my kitchen, waiting to go to my graduation. There's no way he's ruining today. This is my day to get closure on the misery that was high school. Misery that he started.

I slowly reopen my eyelids and blink twice, before checking around the corner. Yep, that's Vlad. He's in my kitchen, scrolling through his phone like he doesn't have a care in the world.

As if he can feel me staring at him, his nostrils flare, and he calls out, "I'll take some juice too, Little Mir."

Vlad is a year and a half older than me, but two grades ahead because of my summer birthday. Ever since he moved to the other side of town, a few years back, he's made comments about how young and small

I am. I may be short and I may be eighteen months younger than Vlad, but neither of those things make me inferior to him. Despite how much he tries to insinuate they do.

Ignoring his request, I remove one glass from the cabinet and pour orange juice for myself, with the fridge still open behind me. I move the glass towards my mouth for a sip, but I'm interrupted by a warm form pressing against the back of my body. A shiver passes over me just before Vlad's meaty hand snatches my juice out of my hand.

"Hey!" I cry out, wiggling around trying to angle my body to face him.

Being between Vlad and the granite countertop is like being trapped between two boulders. By the time we're face to face, Vlad has consumed almost the entire glass. He leans forward invading my space, his hot, orangey breath hitting my cheeks and nose. "Thanks for the juice," he whispers with a smirk, revealing his perfect white teeth as he sets the glass on the countertop behind me.

My whole body buzzes like a live wire the second I notice the intimate position we're in. The counter is pressing into the middle of my spine and Vlad's warm body is plastered against my front as he towers over me. My cheeks heat as he tilts his face closer, skimming his nose across my forehead. A small strangled noise escapes my lips at the touch. Part fear and part... something else.

Abruptly, Vlad steps back and returns to his spot in

the kitchen nook. He whips his phone out of his pocket and continues scrolling like nothing happened.

Seconds later, whistling announces my dad as he rounds the corner, entering the kitchen. He pats my head as he strolls to the fridge. "Hey kiddo, ready for your big day?"

A response is on the tip of my tongue when Vlad hops up from the bench again. "Hey, Mr. Love."

"Vlad!" My dad exclaims, sounding ten times more thrilled to see him than he was to see me.

For whatever reason, adults never seem to see Vlad as the big fat... er fit, bully that he is. Everyone loves Vlad. When our families go somewhere together, he walks around bro hugging every guy in sight, while girls fawn all over him.

It's disgusting.

Tuning out their conversation, I place Vlad's used glass in the dishwasher and grab another for my juice. There's no way I'm sharing with Vlad. He probably has massive amounts of germs floating around in his saliva.

THE UNIVERSE IS CONSPIRING against me.

Apparently, the discussion I studiously ignored ended with the agreement that Vlad would drive me to graduation. No amount of protesting could convince my dad, and the later addition of my mom, otherwise.

Both of my parents are firmly team Vlad.

Outside, I force myself to clamber into his silly sports car, as my giddy parents and an indifferent seeming Vlad watch on. He revs the engine the second my butt hits the stupid leather seat. He taps his foot as I settle myself, appearing eager to get this over with. As soon as the dumb metal clip of the seatbelt locks, he zips off down the road, leaving my parents behind in the driveway.

Sneaking my phone out of the plastic bag I stuffed my cap and gown into, I shoot Sylvia an urgent text message with one word: **SOS.**

It comforts me when she messages back immediately: **What happened?**

My nerves flare as I rethink the situation. What if Vlad driving me is a rouse to get me alone before my big day? What if he did this for a chance to ruin my dress? Flashes of the movie Carrie suddenly surge forward in my brain. Then I become paranoid he might dump some type of liquid on me in his car.

My thumbs fly across the screen as I finally type my response: **Parents made me ride with Vlad, prepare for worst case scenario. Bring backup dress. PLEASE.**

Instead of waiting for Sylvia's reply, I shove my phone back into the plastic bag and seal it tightly shut. Hopefully, it will stay safe in there, away from whatever Vlad has planned.

"Do you mind if we stop for coffee?" Vlad asks in a polite tone.

Shock over his manners filters through my system, slightly delaying my response. "Uh, I think we should head straight there..." I trail off as he swerves his car towards a drive-up coffee stand, ignoring me.

Of course, Vlad would do what he wants regardless of my response. The stand he chose is essentially a small shack appearing large enough to hold one or two people and serve coffee through the window.

Coffee is an art form in the Northwest, and you can find it on almost every corner. Our town is modest in size and we have three coffee stands plus an actual coffee shop on each side of the Main Road, downtown. I've never been to this particular stand before, but I'm also not a huge coffee drinker.

There's only one car ahead of us, but they must have a complicated order because the wait is lengthy. We both remain silent, Vlad's obnoxiously loud engine the only audible noise, and my impatience mounts with each second that passes.

I begin to lightly tap my fingers on my knee, wondering what type of torture Vlad has planned for me next. Tipping forward to look out the window, I eye the sign for the stand. The billboard features the silhouette of a busty girl bent in half with a steaming cup of coffee placed on her outstretched palm.

The car in front of us finally leaves, and Vlad slowly rolls forward, capturing my attention again. I watch as he slowly lowers his window, at the same speed as the car drifting forward. The second we stop, an excited, feminine voice squeals, "Vlaaaaad!"

I glance up and immediately see a barely clothed girl jumping up and down, her giant chest flopping around with the movement. The barista is barely dressed, her huge boobs shoved into a sheer bra. Her modesty protected by a set of tiny pasties and a g-string.

My entire face burns and I quickly turn away, blushing furiously after catching only a glimpse of the girl. I didn't comprehend the meaning behind the bill-board until seeing the barista.

Vlad brought me to the lingerie coffee stand on the other side of the Main Road!

"Why didn't you call me the other day?" The girl whines at Vlad, her familiarity startling.

I ignore their conversation and my mind wanders as I avoid looking at the mostly naked barista. Is Vlad a regular at this coffee stand? Or does he know the barista from somewhere else? Actually, why do I even care?

Vlad is the worst.

I personally can't understand what anyone sees in him. Sure, he's good looking, I guess. Tall and broad with dark hair and classic features. I might see the physical attraction, but there's more to life than looks and Vlad's personality sucks. He's a total jerk!

Have some standards, barista girl.

Vlad twists to face me, interrupting my thoughts as he asks, "What would you like, Little Mir?"

Startled, I turn, eyeing his blank expression with suspicion. "Nothing," I finally reply cautiously. "I had juice at the house."

Vlad doesn't react to my words, other than to stare

me down. I break eye contact first, switching my gaze to the window and ignoring Vlad and the barista once more.

A few moments later, the sound of two drinks plopping into the cup holders in quick succession jolts me. I glance at Vlad's expressionless face, then the two coffee cups before moving my eyes to the scenery now blurring past the window.

He tries to engage me in conversation a few times during the twenty-minute car ride, but I refuse to speak. I continue staring out the window like I haven't lived in this town my entire life and I don't want to miss any of the views.

I don't touch the coffee Vlad says is mine. He knew the barista. Who knows what he had her do to my drink? It's probably filled with ex-lax or siracha or something else equally nefarious, intended to ruin my day. He may have my parents and most of the town fooled, but there's no way I'll ever forget that Vlad opened the floodgates for my tormentors in high school. It'll be a cold day in hell before I accept anything edible from him.

It feels like five hours have passed when we finally arrive at my high school where the graduation ceremony is commencing. I leap out of Vlad's car just as his arm nears my body and a light pat touches my back.

I yell, "Thank you." Then rush out of the car, not waiting for his response, snagging my belongings as I exit. Without a backward glance, I scurry towards the entrance to find the pre-ceremony meeting area.

3

THE CEREMONY

Mirabella

I'm forced to weave through a crowd, dodging parents and students as they swoop towards each other for hellos. While winding through the mob, I unzip my bag to grab my phone.

Clicking on the screen, I spot alerts for thirty-five messages from Sylvia. Scrolling through her texts I see they start out easy going: **Hope he's not too much of an ass.** But steadily become more concerned and aggressive, finally ending with: **I WILL CALL THE COPS IF YOU DON'T TEXT ME BACK IMME-DIATELY.**

My fingers zip over the glass as I type my response. My eyes entirely focused on my phone and my thoughts preoccupied with reassuring my friend, I'm distracted from the walkway in front of me.

It's a rookie mistake.

Someone takes advantage of my distraction to shove me from behind. I fall hard on the cement ground, barely raising my hands in time to prevent a broken nose. A loud "oomph" escapes from my body upon impact, as my palms skid across the pavement.

Laughter floats down from all sides, a sure sign the incident was intentional. Pushing myself up onto my knees, I grab at the hem of my dress to ensure I'm covered. Remaining hunched over, I conduct a brief self-inspection, checking for injuries.

My nose remains intact from my quick reaction. Unfortunately, my phone was not as lucky and now sports an enormous crack across the center of the screen. As I turn it over in my hands, I find a spot of blood and realize my right palm is also bleeding. Sighing, I place the phone back into my bag and cradle my hand. Then, without raising my head fully, I formulate an exit strategy to avoid my tormentors lingering nearby.

My ears perk as I hear Sylvia's voice. "Move out of my way," she screeches viciously.

An angry Sylvia is not to be trifled with and the shuffling of feet informs me students are quickly scattering to clear her path. Within seconds, I feel her hovering over me. "Are you okay, Mira?"

The second her shoes come into view, I glance up and meet her concerned brown gaze. "Yeah I think so," I reply uncertainly. Behind her, I see the crowd continuing to disperse, bored with the scene since the round of Mira torture is over. At least for now.

"Come on, let's get you cleaned up," she responds, offering her hand to assist me.

I hiss when her palm connects with mine, putting pressure on the minor cut. She raises a brow, but doesn't comment. Sylvia simply leads me to a bathroom nearby.

Sylvia has a sixth sense that alerts her when I'm in trouble. From day one, whenever I need her most, she arrives at the perfect time to save me. My tormentors tried to pick on her too, but they quickly moved onto easier prey when their taunts didn't stick. Her carefree attitude seems like a front at first glance, but Sylvia really doesn't care about anyone else's opinion of her.

Sylvia's also gorgeous. She's a half foot taller than me, like almost everyone else, with hair that changes color every few months. Right now it's bright blue, twisted into a French braid ending just past her shoulders. To complete her graduation look, she's wearing a black dress, heavy black eyeliner, and heeled doc martens. On anyone else, her outfit would look ridiculous, but on Sylvia it looks trendy and artistic, rather than gothic.

Some days, I wish I could be more like her.

If I hadn't cared about the opinions of my bullies, maybe high school would have been different. Instead, I tried to play nice and accepted blame for things that weren't my fault. It wasn't until I met Sylvia that I stood up for myself, and by then it was a little too late.

Shaking my head to clear my thoughts, I dig out the pieces of gravel pitting my hands, then run my palms under the water. While the cool liquid soothes the minor injury, I inspect my appearance. I survived the fall relatively unscathed. My bright blue dress, the same color as Sylvia's hair, remains clean and intact. The hairstyle my mom created, with loose curls and a crown braid, also appears to be fine.

My gaze lands on my face and I see my smudged mascara from the stray tears that escaped during my fall. Meeting Sylvia's gaze in the mirror, I ask, "Can you fix this?" Then point to my eyes, in the general direction of the mascara disaster.

With a nod, she whips out some makeup and places it on the countertop. Grabbing a paper towel, she swipes under my eyes, then grabs her eyeliner. "Hold still for a sec," she says, gripping my chin.

I remain still as a statue, worried if I move a muscle, I'll mess something up. Seconds later, she steps back and gives a cheeky, "Voila!" She brandishes her hand in the air, presenting me to myself.

Giving another cursory glance in the mirror, I smile, pleased with the results. "Thanks, Syl. We should probably head back out there to wait with everyone else."

I pivot, intending to exit the bathroom, but Sylvia stops me. Placing a hand on my shoulder, she holds me still. "What's this on your back, Mira?"

Craning my neck, I attempt to see over my shoulder. Did Sylvia find a stain on my dress from the fall? "I can't see anything," I huff in frustration, giving up on being able to contort my body and see my back.

Sylvia grabs at something, causing the fabric of my dress to tug against me with the movement. I hear what sounds like tape peeling, then she wordlessly hands it to me over the top of my shoulder.

I snatch it from her hands, surprised when I see it's a picture. My shoulders slump the second I realize it's a photo of me standing in the doorway to the locker room with a towel clutched around my body. I look like a drowned cat with my wet, scraggly hair dripping down my body and puddling on the floor.

The image is from two weeks ago when my clothes went missing, again, while I was showering after gym class. I remember the incident clearly. I spotted the girls and chased them partway out of the locker room. They were sprinting away, and I was scared to wander too far in a towel. My clothes weren't recovered, and I had to wear old, smelly gym clothes for the rest of the day.

"Hmmm," Sylvia says. "Why don't we just hang out in here until it's time for the ceremony? We can just glob onto the end of the group. Who cares if we sit near the back, anyway?"

I nod, eyes still fixated on the photograph, replaying the events of this morning in my head. "Vlad put this on me! He patted my back as I was leaving the car," I finally exclaim.

Outrage replaces defeat. I'm pissed at Vlad for his stupid prank, but also mad at myself for thinking he wouldn't try something today. I should've come straight to the bathroom after leaving his car to check myself. Someday I'll make Vlad pay. He'll suffer the same way I have since I was twelve years old.

"What an asshat." Sylvia commiserates, interrupting my unspoken promise of revenge. She's already set up camp in the bathroom, lounging against one of the stalls. I watch as she pulls a cigarette from her purse and lights it with a neon green zippo. I silently observe as she inhales a deep drag then sends puffs of smoke into the air and immediately begins coughing.

I stifle a laugh, turning it into a cough as she aims a glare in my direction. Sylvia turned eighteen during the school year and likes to pretend she smokes now. I rarely see her do it, but when I do, she's terrible at it.

"Agreed." I join Sylvia against the stall, the cool metal penetrating my dress as my thoughts wander. Sylvia snatches the photo from my hand and crumples it into a ball, chucking it into the garbage bin.

Silence permeates the air for a few brief seconds, then Sylvia stubs out her cigarette and randomly says, "My youngest brother has started stealing underwear to pretend they're superhero masks."

"What?" I ask, giggling and immediately forgetting about Vlad the terrible.

"Yeah, I swear he's going through the laundry and snatching them up. At least they're clean I guess, but he woke me up yesterday screaming that he needed to save me from a monster underneath my bed with a thong draped over his face."

"Oh my gosh," I wheeze out between giggles. "Your brothers are so weird."

She chuckles and nods, "You're telling me."

An announcement breaks through our laughter from the school-wide speakers. "Students, please report to the auditorium."

Sighing, I push away from the stall and trail behind Sylvia as she strides purposefully towards the door. I attempt to mimic her posture, straightening my spine and squaring my shoulders as we join the rest of the seniors. There are two high schools in town, so our graduating class is tiny, with only about seventy or so students.

Teachers herd us like sheep, keeping an orderly line as we file through the center towards the front. Standing on my tiptoes, I see the stage has risers on the left and a small podium for speeches on the right.

The sight fortifies me. I'm about to leave this place behind and start the next chapter of my life.

Despite the teachers corralling us, a wave of laughter begins at the front of the line, slowly trickling down. At first, I don't realize why it's happening and shrug my shoulders as I continue to trudge forward. It isn't until the line slows to a stop and fingers point to the sides that I stop to inspect my surroundings.

All around the auditorium, the chairs have pictures taped against the back. The images are slightly visible from the aisle and my stomach fills with dread. Ignoring the teacher posted at the edge of the nearest row, I step out of line and grab the closest photo for confirmation.

Anxiety and embarrassment flood my veins and the image flutters to the ground as my fingers go slack. I surge forward, snatching a photo off of each chair, glancing at it, before rushing through the rest of the row with mania.

Each image is of me. Each one more embarrassing than the last.

Every prank I've survived during my high school career has been photographed and taped to the back of a chair. One after another, terrible memories of high school overwhelm me and my eyes flood with tears.

Mid-itch a tiiiny bit inside my nose, clay smattering my body after leaving my class at the community center, the day my pants split last year, the time I sat in red paint and everyone said it was period blood. Photo after photo of my life plastered onto the chairs for everyone in town to see.

I leave the rest of the pictures and hurry from the room. Normally, I don't allow my classmates to witness my defeat, but this is too much. My family will see these, the whole town will laugh at my humiliation. The hope of a fresh start after graduation has officially been destroyed.

Graduation means nothing.

I burst through the doors with tears streaming down my face and a wad of photographs clutched in my hand. Part of me wishes this day was over, or this stupid ceremony didn't exist, but I know my classmates would've found another way to convey their message: they'll never stop. A commotion starts behind me, but I don't glance back. Sprinting into the courtyard with my gown billowing behind me, I run straight into a warm wall of solid muscle.

An "oomph" escapes my body for the second time today and I screw my eyes shut in preparation of hitting the ground. Instead of connecting with the cement, a pair of powerful arms catch me around the waist. I open one eyelid, slowly, to see my savior.

Vlad's smirking face comes into focus and I release a frustrated exhale. Of course, it's him, here to gloat over his successful torture. I'm positive this was his plan.

Stepping out of his hold, I level him with the angriest glare I can muster. My eyes are red and puffy and tears carry makeup down my face in rivulets, but that doesn't stop me from laying into him. "You're a real piece of work, and I hope you die." I shove the photos against his chest and walk past him to my parents. Softening my tone, I ask, "Can you take me home? I... uh, don't feel well."

My parents exchange a look, then my dad wraps an arm around my shoulders, squeezing me into his side. "Are you sure, Kiddo? You only get one high school graduation! I don't want you to miss your chance."

I nod my head slowly. "Yeah Dad, I'm sure."

Keeping his grip on my shoulders, he steers me to the parking lot. "Ookay," he drawls. "This is your day. We can spend it however you'd like, kiddo."

My mom weaves her arm around my shoulder, winding it underneath my dad's. Together, the three of us walk away from a frozen Vlad and an auditorium full of shame, towards the parking lot.

My parents say nothing else. They don't make a fuss about leaving or press me to find out what happened. It's one of the things I love the most about them. They give me room to make my own decisions and offer their support when necessary.

Once I get in the car, I take a deep, calming breath and try to think of all the exceptional things that I've been gifted in this life. My parents, Sylvia, my art. I feel my resolve strengthening with each positive thought. A layer of armor placed around my battered body with each affirmation I provide myself.

Yes, Vlad won today, but someday the torment will end. For now, nothing he does can steal the things important to me.

4

THE PAINTING

Mirabella

The car brakes, I shake myself from my thoughts, and unbuckle. I'm surprised when I glance out the window and see the ice cream parlor instead of our house. My dad opens my door, and announces gravely, "It's an important rite of passage for any high school graduate to eat ice cream the day of their graduation."

I groan, but I'm secretly thankful he thought of the treat. Stopping by the parlor to get ice cream after graduation seems like such a normal thing for a recent grad to do. The idea makes the rest of the day a little less terrible.

"Wait for just one second," my mom commands. I remain in my seat, watching as she pulls a makeup wipe from her purse. "Close your eyes," she instructs.

I obey and feel her wipe the cool cloth across my

face to fix my makeup. I'm sure my crying bout left my face a mess. When she finishes, I hear her step away and my eyes snap open.

"Thanks, mom," I say a little sheepishly.

"Anytime, sweetie. Now let's go get some ice cream," She replies, a smile gracing her heart-shaped face as she waits for me to join her on the curb. When I step out, she links our arms, dragging me with her as she takes long strides.

Inside, the Parlor is empty and my mom quickly disconnects our arms to press against the glass shield. The one that protects the ice cream from people like her that feel the need to hover. I smile at her antics. Mom's sweet tooth is terrible, but she rarely gives into her urges to indulge in sugary delights.

The teenage girl behind the counter approaches my mom first, sensing she's most anxious to order. "What can I get you?"

My mom points at the glass. "Can I get a scoop of that one?" As the girl scoops from the specified container, my mom walks a few steps further down the counter. "Ooh, and that one?" The girl scoops the next flavor, and my mom walks away once more. "Oh, and this one too?" she asks, excitedly.

I giggle as my dad intercepts her, stopping the madness prior to my mom creating a cone with twelve scoops of ice cream. "Okay, Rebecca. We should let Mira order, since it's her graduation. After that we can get a pint to go, if you want more."

My mom looks crestfallen until the girl behind the

counter passes her the gigantic ice cream cone. "This is probably enough ice cream for now," she agrees on a laugh, taking a bite off the side.

The girl works quickly to scoop and serve cones for my dad and I, next. Within minutes, we're strolling outside to enjoy our cones at one of the bistro tables on the sidewalk.

"Oh, Mira. Let me take a few pictures of you in your cap and gown," My mom exclaims before I'm able to eat my cone. She digs a small camera out of her purse and I hear the camera click, as she snaps a few shots of me posing, cone still in hand.

After five or six, she finally declares, "These are adorable!" She puts the camera on the table, quickly forgotten as she focuses on her ice cream.

I devour my cone faster than both of my parents, then tap my fingers on the table until an idea pops into my head. "Can I use the camera?" I ask, without explaining my intentions.

My mom nods, too busy devouring her cone to speak. Picking up the slim, black camera, I play around for a few seconds then snap a few photos of my parents eating their cones together. They laugh good-naturedly and move their heads closer together for a better shot.

I love my parents.

They're high school sweethearts still in love, with one another and with their lives. I think their love story is the reason that they're so insistent about Vlad and I becoming a couple. My parents can't see how evil he is because they think we'll end up like them.

I'm about to hand the camera back when my dad chants, "Usie, Usie, Usie."

I'm about to hand the camera back when my dad chants, "Usie, Usie, Usie."

I groan over his wannabe hip language, when my parents are still taking pictures with a camera instead of a cell phone, but oblige him anyway. Facing the camera towards us, I position the lens and snap a shot of the three of us, our heads crammed together.

ICE CREAM with my parents lifted some of my despair, and I already feel lighter by the time my dad parks in the garage. After I stride into my room and deposit my cap and gown, I read through a stream of messages from Sylvia, updating me on the graduation ceremony I missed.

Sylvia: **After you left, all the risers collapsed.** I gasp, then continue reading: **We weren't on stage yet, so no one got hurt... Although maybe it wouldn't have been too terrible if Kaylee had been up there.**

I nod at her sentiment regarding my main tormentor, then scan her next message: **We've all been evacuated. Sneaking back in to clean up photos.**

My eyebrows raise in shock as she continues giving me a play-by-play: **Vlad the asshat snuck in too. HE'S CLEANING UP WITH ME.**

Wait, what? Why would he be cleaning up with Sylvia? That doesn't make sense. Maybe he wasn't behind the prank? Or maybe he didn't care to leave the photos behind, since I was already humiliated and he didn't want to get caught? The second option seems more likely, just because it's Vlad.

The mystery of Vlad's actions solved, I read the last message: **They caught us, but we cleaned up most of them. They also can't fix the risers, so now graduation is in the cafeteria. Honestly, you aren't missing much. This whole thing is a shit show.**

I laugh and type back a quick response: **Thank you. For updates and photo disposal. Going to paint, I'll ttyl.** Throwing my phone on the bed, I retreat to my art studio in the next room.

It's my favorite space in our entire house. Sometimes I think my mom is disappointed that I don't love dressing up and doing my makeup as much as she does. I tolerate clothes shopping with her as much as I can and always wear the new clothes she gets me. I'm just not passionate about fashion like she is.

I would much rather be in a pair of paint-stained jeans, flinging paint in the studio my dad built me. Nothing else compares to the feeling of covering a canvas in colorful artwork.

With a deep inhale, my eyes scan my oasis. My dad built shelving units against one wall that house my paints, brushes, smocks, and blank canvases. In the corner closest to the door, there's two oversized leather chairs. I also have a sink off to the far side, with some counter space beside it for washing and drying my tools. It's convenient for me, but also greatly appreciated by my mom, since I don't have to trek through the house with paint-covered items. In addition to the supplies, four permanent easels are set up throughout the room with a raised dais in the center, in case I ever have a live subject. There are two large windows near the sink to provide natural light, but my dad also installed special ceiling lamps that mimic sunlight. Most of the wall space that isn't taken by windows is now covered in my art.

As I glance around my studio, the urge to create begins pulsing through my fingertips. I'm still in my graduation outfit, so I kick off my heels, snagging a smock to throw over my dress.

Grabbing a random assortment of colors, I prep one of my easels to paint. Then, I connect my iPod to a small speaker nearby and press play. With music oozing into the space, I get in the zone. Dancing, singing, and slinging paint. I rarely plan what I want to appear on my canvas. I just let it happen. Today is no different, as I allow my creativity to flow through me and onto the blank space before me.

When the image is fully formed, with every inch of previously blank canvas now covered in color, I step back. Tilting my head to the side, I examine the painting.

A large, black wolf is running through the forest with his head turned back to the viewer. A few other wolves are in the picture with him, but their features aren't as clear. They're simply blurs racing amongst the trees. The wolf in focus has intelligent amber eyes, he seems to enjoy the run, but paused to look over his shoulder at the unknown.

Wolves have been one of my favorite subjects to paint for probably the last four or five years. An entire wall in my studio is currently dedicated to completed wolf paintings. Something about the subject fascinates me and I love how versatile they are to paint.

Tilting my head in the opposite direction, I study my newest wolf painting for a few more seconds. Something about the amber eyes look familiar.

Almost like... Vlad's.

I shake my head and turn away. Leaving the canvas on the easel to dry, I walk to the sink to rinse off my brushes.

Thoughts of Vlad pop into my head unbidden too often and I hate it.

5

THE OPPORTUNITY

Mirabella

Scratch paper litters my desk, covered with bits of advice written in my scrawling script. I've spent the entire day in my room, Foogle searching through potential interview questions, to prepare for this afternoon. As of now, I don't have an interview, but I'm optimistic that when I go to the library and apply, they'll offer me a position on the spot. At the very least, I'd like to be prepared in case they conduct a brief interview today.

During the days since Sunday dinner, I've reconsidered working at the Daily alongside Vlad. In the heat of the moment, being an intern sounded like a good idea, but the more I've thought about it, the more it seems like a mistake. It would be so satisfying to get revenge on Vlad in his workplace, but in reality, it's more likely he would just torture me and ruin my reputation instead. On top of that, anything either of us did would happen in front of the town's most notorious gossips: the staff of the Daily.

The last thing I want is a prank gone wrong to become front page news.

Both our parents were elated about us working together at the Daily. In order to avoid a scene, I plan to break my decision to them gently, later. If I get the job at the library, I can relay the good and bad news all at once and avoid making them too upset.

A knock on my door interrupts my online search and I holler, "Come in!" I twirl in my chair without bothering to stand.

My dad steps into my bedroom, hovering close to the door, but wearing a broad smile. "Hey dad, what's up?" I ask after we stare each other down for a few seconds.

"I talked to Marc today!" He's looking at me eagerly with happiness shining in his gray gaze, like I should dance joyfully at his announcement, but I'm unsure why.

"Ookay," I draw out, waiting to hear why he's smiling like a loon.

"He agreed to give you an internship at the *F.O. Daily*!" He blurts out, throwing two jazz hands in front of him, like he's a game show host announcing I won a new car.

It takes a few seconds for his words to sink in. When they do, the floor feels like it drops out from underneath me. How could he have already volunteered me for the internship? How could I already be hired? I agreed to the idea less than seventy-two hours ago.

I thought I would have time to change my mind, to interview at the library, and let my parents down gently. No one, except the people at our dinner table on Sunday night, would ever need to know that I considered an internship at the Daily. How could he do this to me?

I'm panic-shouting questions in my mind when I realize my dad is still excitedly talking about the internship opportunity.

"I don't want to do it!" I shriek, cutting my dad off mid-sentence. Inhaling a deep breath, I repeat in a much calmer and quieter tone, "I mean, I thought more about it and I've come to the decision that the library would be a better fit for me."

"Mira." Even just saying my name, he sounds disappointed. His tone makes me wish I could open my mouth and stuff my previous words back into it. My dad is always on my team and I hate thinking he might not agree with my decision. "You can't bail out now. You've already committed. They're counting on you to show up next Monday as their intern."

"But I didn't commit, you committed for me," I protest weakly.

My mom pops her head around the door, peering into the room. "What're you two plotting in here?" She asks, a wide grin on her face.

My dad faces her, still speaking in his crestfallen

tone. "I went to talk to Marc at the Daily today. He agreed to give Mira the internship position..." My dad pauses briefly, allowing my mom to finish her excited clap without missing his next words. "I came to give Mira the exciting news, but she insists the library is a better fit."

"Ohh Mira," my mom exclaims, sounding ten times more disappointed than my dad.

These two are really laying it on thick over an internship I just decided that I maybe wanted a few nights ago.

My mom continues, "No one likes a quitter. Take the opportunity and run with it before making the decision to quit. They're counting on you now. It wouldn't be fair to change your mind after they've already given you the position."

I offer a small nod to acknowledge her words. At this point, there's no use arguing. When my parents gang up on me, I always lose. Sighing, I relent, "I guess I'll be the intern at the *F.O. Daily.*"

I silently add, "Now I have to spend my entire summer with Vlad freaking Mort," and imagining my parent's reaction if I said the words aloud.

DESPITE MY ATTEMPTS TO ignore it, the end of the week looms closer each day. I feel my freedom slowly slipping between my fingertips. As a distraction, I spend the time before my internship alternating between painting and hanging out with Sylvia. Or sometimes, painting while I hang out with Sylvia. We don't have much free time left this summer to spend together.

By Sunday, I'm essentially a tightly wound ball of dread. The last few hours of freedom, before I'm forced to spend eight hours a day, five days a week with Vlad, are closing in around me like a vice. Painting is helping to relieve some of my tension, as is Sylvia's presence and chatter, but nothing can dissipate it completely.

With one last swipe of my paintbrush, my entire canvas becomes coated in a layer of paint. I stride away, heading to the sink to rinse my brushes out. My eyes flit to Sylvia lounging in one of the leather armchairs scrolling through her social media, but she doesn't notice. Music is blasting through my mini speaker and I roll my shoulders, attempting to relieve some soreness setting into my muscles after hours of painting.

When I reach the sink, Sylvia's voice startles me. I twirl around to respond, only to see she's yelling at her phone. Apparently, things have become heated as she argues with someone on a post about whether straws are the primary killer of ocean animals. Her commentary becomes a steady stream of background noise as I rinse off my brushes. "You're a fucking Idiot, Casey! What about sport fishing or oil spills? Paper straws will not save the ocean, dickhead."

Her rant is a bit of comedic relief from my preoccupied thoughts of Vlad. Anxiety and fear have slowly built in my chest all day. I keep imagining different scenarios Vlad could incite, embarrassing me in front of my new coworkers, all while appearing an innocent bystander.

Once my brushes are clean, I look at Sylvia. She seems content just to hang out in the studio today, so I grab another canvas to paint. I choose black as my first color and sketch outlines in light strokes. Humming, I darken some spaces before moving to a new color.

After an hour or so, I notice the room is unusually quiet. My playlist must've run out of songs. I pause my painting to address Sylvia, but her gaze is fixated on my canvas. I've been painting without paying much attention to my creation, so I'm unsure why she's so transfixed. Stepping back, I look.

My painting features an office with desks scattered about in a semi-organized fashion, enough places to seat about twenty. The large pieces of furniture are the only thing that look even slightly arranged within the room. Chairs are on their sides with their wheels up in the air, people are huddling under desks, and an ominous, dark figure stands behind a small tornado of papers twirling amidst the chaos in the room.

Sylvia's arms wrap around me from behind as she offers a "hmm." She rests her chin atop my head, continuing to examine my painting with me. "It won't be that bad, Mir. He works there too, like as an actual job, not just as an intern. He won't risk ruining his own reputation just to play a dumb prank on you."

I pat her arm and nod. It's enough to reassure her, even though I disagree with her statement. Sylvia's been my support system for years. She's seen the aftereffects of Vlad's pranks and comforted me at my lowest points. I can't tell if she believes her own words or wants me to approach the situation with a positive attitude and hope for the best. Choosing to believe the latter, her words provide little comfort.

The moment ends and Sylvia returns to her chair, picking up her phone and resuming whatever argument she's moved on to now. I turn my music back on, allowing myself to eye my painting for a couple more seconds, before placing the canvas to the side to dry. Walking to the sink, I rinse out my brushes again and grab a blank slate, placing it on my easel.

I try to fixate on more positive thoughts as I resume painting.

6

THE INTERN

Mirabella

Mira, hurry up kiddo. You're going to be late," my dad yells down the hall, startling me from a deep sleep.

I grapple for my phone, groaning at the brightness of the screen shining in my tired eyes. Adrenaline hits and I shoot upright, once the time registers. I overslept and need to be at the Daily in half an hour. My first day as an intern and I'm about to be late.

I jump out of bed, frantic and unsure how this happened. I could've sworn I set two alarms last night before crawling into bed. Maybe I dreamt the alarms?

Scrambling around my room, I throw my hair into a quick ponytail and snatch up a navy-blue pencil skirt and a white blouse. I know next to nothing about my new job, including the specifics of the dress code, and I don't have time to question my outfit. Business casual seems like a safe bet for my first day, at least I won't be underdressed.

Once I'm clothed, I run downstairs to grab coffee and a banana, then rush to my Prius, throwing myself in the seat. With one slow, calming breath, I buckle and cautiously back down my driveway, hoping I'm not late.

Luckily, the Daily starts earlier than most of the other businesses, so traffic is light. With three minutes to spare, I park my car at the *F.O Daily*, quickly hopping out and hustling inside. I'm careful to avoid spilling coffee on my white blouse, already regretting wearing the easy-to-stain color on my first day. In a place that I'll be working with Vlad, no less.

The reception area is empty upon entering. I peek past the front desk and see a sizable group in a circle near the back of the massive room. Some people have chairs, while others are standing about. Not wanting to miss anything, I invite myself to join the cluster.

As I reach the gathering, a handsome, light-haired gentleman who looks to be in his mid-twenties approaches me. "Are you Mirabella?" He asks. At my nod, he continues. "I'm Marc. I spoke with your father about the internship opportunity here. We're excited to have you onboard." He extends a hand and offers a wolfish grin.

Marc is quite handsome, with pearly white teeth and brilliant gem-colored eyes. Shaking his hand, I notice his palms are warm and smooth without the calluses that mar Vlad's. "Nice to meet you, Marc," I reply, berating myself for letting my mind wander to thoughts of my nemesis.

Similar to saying Beetlejuice three times, mentally thinking of Vlad seems to summon him. He suddenly appears nearby, angrily glaring at me with his corded arms crossed against his broad chest, watching while I speak with Marc.

Ignoring him, I focus on my conversation. "Thank you for offering me the internship. I'm really excited to learn more about the Daily. Oh, and you can call me Mira." I continue, returning his genuine smile with a small one of my own.

"Mira." Marc repeats, rolling my name around in his mouth, testing it out. "Great to have you here. We're about to start our morning meeting where everyone pitches story ideas and assignments are divided out." He gestures to the small crowd next to us, quietly chatting as they wait for the meeting to commence. "Feel free to stand or pull up a chair."

I murmur a quiet "thank you" and Marc returns to the front of the semi-circle.

He claps his hands together twice. "Alright, let's get started. Before we get into it, I want to introduce the new intern, Mira." He waves a hand in my direction and I suddenly become the focus of fifteen sets of eyes.

I'm still standing by myself in the middle of the room, and I offer a small, awkward wave accompanied by a shy smile. Most everyone waves or smiles back, except for one person, Vlad. He shoots a glare in my direction, but it's not like I expected anything else.

After everyone's gaze returns to the front, I shuffle forward. Joining the group, I remain silent, taking the opportunity to observe the group dynamics of the meeting. The staff politely raises their hands, waiting for Marc to call on them to share their article ideas.

I cringe at some of the story suggestions. Our town is pretty small, and if this meeting is any indication, filling a daily paper is quite the struggle. Marc is very diplomatic about declining the less-than-exciting sounding ideas and offering better ones.

Marc, although younger than quite a few of the staff members, possesses diplomacy and charm. It's clear why he's the man in charge of operations. He seems very passionate about journalism, but also kind and willing to listen, even if he doesn't ultimately agree.

When the whiteboard is full of suggestions, Marc assigns the stories to staff members at random. Once they're divvied up, the meeting ends and people begin to disperse, but Marc stops them. His voice floats over the large room as he states, "I want to assign the intern to shadow someone today. Any volunteers?"

I remain frozen in place, with my fingers crossed behind me, chanting, "Not Vlad, not Vlad, anyone but Vlad," under my breath.

My prayers are answered when an older woman raises her hand. She looks like the Hollywood portrayal of a grandmother, with graying hair knotted in a bun, small glasses perched on her nose, and a modest, loose dress.

Definitely a safer choice than Vlad.

"Alright. Thanks Glenna." Marc acknowledges, officially declaring her my savior.

I hang back as everyone else walks away, waiting to move to avoid fighting through a crowd. Once the path is clear, I stride across the room to introduce myself. "Glenna? I'm Mira. Thank you for letting me shadow you today."

She shakes my hand while she replies in a raspy sounding voice, "Of course, honey. You're going to love covering the knitting expo. It's my favorite time of year."

I barely hold in my groan. The knitting expo?

Our town holds a few expos every year. A knitting expo, a pet expo, and a Christmas expo. The events never change. Honestly, the vendors and products rarely do either, but the people of Florence love the expos. Three years ago, the Mayor was quoted saying he was thinking about changing them. The specifics of the changes weren't even listed in his statement, but his public approval rating tanked. It became so low, he was forced to appear on the local news with a retraction, promising Florence he would never discontinue or change the expos, just so he could stay in office.

The events are a huge news opportunity, so it makes sense the Daily plans to cover the knitting expo in depth. Last year, a famous crochet artist came to sign autographs and things got rowdy. One lady stabbed another with her knitting needle. There were accusations of line cutting—amongst other claims—

that led to the brutality. Both ladies were escorted out of the expo and banned from the venue for the remainder of the event. The Daily's coverage of the story was out of control. Someone snapped a picture of the stabbing and *F.O. Daily* posted it on their front page every day until someone complained about graphic content.

"Do we have to go to the expo today?" I question, attempting to determine how involved I'll need to be.

"Oh no, honey." Glenna chuckles. "The expo isn't for a few weeks. We're just going to write an article reviewing past years and anticipate what products will sell best. If you're lucky, you may get to attend with me, when the time comes."

Her words flood me with relief. In the past, I've avoided the expos like the plague. Too many people and too much gossip, in one crowded place. Knowing my luck, I would end up on the receiving end of cruel pranks, just for showing my face in public.

"Okay, that sounds like an easy story to write," I respond, trailing her steps across the room.

I try to discreetly examine the entire office, while not running into anything or seeming too distracted. The desks are spread in what appears to be a haphazard manner. Two near the front face reception, but behind those, four sit in a square, all facing inward. To the side of those, two desks face the left wall. Behind the grouping of four, the rest of the desks are in three neat rows facing alternating directions.

There's a large gap of space after the last row of

desks, where the whiteboard used for assignments stands. In the back of the room, furthest from the reception area, there's the office that Marc walked into and a door to another area that looks like a conference room. The wall between the two doors hosts a table of coffee supplies and one of those water dispensers with a gallon-sized jug on top.

As I rushed through the lobby, I noticed two doors off to the far side. I'm guessing they provide access to the restroom and break room. Making a mental note to ask Glenna about it later, I drag a chair to her desk and continue listening.

Glenna points to her computer, and instructs, "Open the archives application and type 'Knitting Expo' that should contain all the information you need." She pulls a magazine from her purse, one featuring a couple of celebrities on the cover, and soon becomes engrossed in flipping through the pages.

I follow her directions, and over fifty articles populate. Pulling over a pad and paper, I click on the first one and jot down a few notes. Every now and then I see Glenna circle things in her magazine with a pen. My imagination briefly entertains the idea of the grandma-esque woman next to me taking a quiz to find out who her celebrity husband should be.

The thought causes me to giggle. At the last second, I'm able to turn the sound into a snort and Glenna glances up from her magazine. "Are you okay, honey?"

"Yes," I reply solemnly, hoping my expression doesn't give away my amusement.

Glenna doesn't seem to notice anything awry. After a brief nod, she refocuses on her reading material and resumes flipping through the pages. We spend the rest of the day that way. Glenna catches up on the trends while I create a timeline for the knitting expo.

I linger for a few minutes following the end of the workday, waiting until I see Vlad pack up and head out, before I do the same. Glenna wanders by and says, "You did a great job for a Newsby."

"A what?" I ask, quizzically.

"A news newbie," she explains.

We both chuckle. It leaves me with a sense of calm as I watch her walk towards the exit. Today went surprisingly well, with no Vlad related incidents. Maybe, just maybe, working at the Daily won't be as bad as I expected.

Gathering my belongings and my courage, I head towards the parking lot with crossed fingers, hoping they protect me against Vlad's continued presence.

7

THE INCIDENT

Mirabella

As the weekend approaches, I'm filled with giddy anticipation, for time away from work and to see Sylvia. Her parents kidnapped her earlier this week, forcing her to go on a wilderness retreat to Alaska. She said they were freaking out over her attending beauty school all summer and needed a chance to "disconnect and connect" together. Meaning they're camped out somewhere with no cell reception and only each other for entertainment.

Thinking about having to spend seven days with Sylvia's little brothers and no internet makes me shudder. I would take my internship with Vlad over that, any day of the week. Although it would be nice if neither of us were stuck in the woods, so I could talk about my internship.

Most of my week has consisted of shadowing

Glenna and writing articles about the knitting expo. Marc also has me training with the receptionist, so I can fill her position when she leaves for vacation in two weeks. So far, my internship has been great.

Only one dark cloud shrouds my time at the Daily.

Vlad.

Every time he walks near me, I make a hasty escape to avoid any pranks he may have up his sleeve. Either he's biding his time or my plan has been working because I've been incident free, so far. Although I don't miss the torment, I'm worried about letting my guard down. It will only make it worse when Vlad finally strikes again. And I'm confident that he will. Strike again, that is.

As I change out the water dispenser jug on Friday, my concerns over Vlad continue to plague. I sense someone's eyes on me and have a sneaking suspicion it's him, but I ignore the feeling. I'm hoping I can complete my task, as part of receptionist training, without incident.

With some shimmying and dramatic maneuvering, I'm able to replace the empty, light canister, with the full jug of water, as requested. By the time it's in place, a light sheen of sweat coats my body from the exertion. I'm hoping the receptionist handles the water dispenser before she leaves, so I don't have to do this again.

Checking the instructions she provided, I skim my finger down the page to find the next step, "Check to ensure working properly". Without looking, I stick my hand out to the side to snag a cup of water, but my fingertips skim someone's T-shirt instead. "Oh, sorry —" I begin, cutting myself off when my eyes latch onto Vlad's amber gaze.

He offers me a cup, a slight smirk settled on his face. Ignoring his offering (what if he poked a hole in the bottom?), I stretch my arm out, as far as possible, to reach around him. Instead of backing off over my obvious disinterest, Vlad takes a few steps closer, situating himself in my line of site on the opposite side of the jug.

Lounging against the wall with his hands in his pockets, Vlad looks like he belongs on the cover of a magazine. He's effortlessly chic in his dark jeans and white tee, both complemented by his broody amber eyes.

Releasing a sigh, I meet his gaze directly. He's been successful in ensuring I can't ignore him without being obviously rude in front of the entire office. This place is loaded with gossipmongers that constantly have an ear to the ground for anything scandalous. Despite the work continuing around us, I know at least one person is paying attention to our interaction and I'm forced to address his presence.

Resigned, I grind out, "Hi Vlad, how can I help you?"

Waiting for his response, I jiggle the cooler, ensuring the jug is firmly in place. Vlad replies loudly to be heard over the noise, "I wanted to talk at your graduation, but you ran off and have been avoiding me. You didn't even join family dinner last week."

Sylvia was over last Sunday, and my parents let us order a pizza and hang out in my studio. Their leniency surprised me. Usually they're adamant about my attendance at dinner with the Morts, but maybe they decided to treat me more like a grownup.

I consider his words, formulating my response while I situate my cup under the spigot and press down. My words are quickly replaced with a shriek as water sprays outwards in a straight line, like it's coming from a fire hydrant instead of an office water cooler.

I remove my hand from the button thinking it will solve the problem, but water continues flooding out after I release it. The gallon jug makes a glugging noise as it rapidly empties its contents onto the two of us and the office floor. Panicking, I glance around for something, anything, to stop the flow of water.

My head whips around, as frantic energy builds in my chest and my hands spasm like the motion will summon a solution straight to my palms. Next to me, Vlad jumps into action. He rips the jug out, placing it gently on the ground. I watch as the water sinks to the bottom of the container and the spray turns into a drizzle, as the last bit of water drains out of the spigot.

Only seconds passed between the spray and Vlad's intervention, but it was long enough to cause damage. The burgundy carpet where we stand is soaked and my clothes are plastered to my body. Vlad is equally sodden, his white shirt and dark jeans clinging to his form. Once my eyes skim down his see-through shirt, I can't look away. Vlad has gotten buff.

When we were kids, he was scrawny. We both were. He rapidly outgrew me in height as we aged, but he was still skinny when our friendship ended. Through his wet shirt, the outline of at least six abs and a pair of defined pecs is visible. Drinking in his muscles, my eyes drift downwards to peruse his thick and muscular thighs, filling his dark jeans nicely as they cling to his skin.

A throat clearing in the background interrupts my perusal of water-soaked Vlad. I glance to my left, and my eyes land on Marc. He's holding his sweatshirt in my direction, with his gaze averted. Glancing down, I find the outline of my blue bra is now fully visible through my soaked shirt. Blushing, I snatch the sweatshirt from Marc, muttering a low "thank you" before tugging it over my head.

When I reemerge, Marc gestures to the two of us. "My office, please." Hanging my head to hide my embarrassment, I trail behind Vlad and enter the office.

This is it.

Vlad must have been planning this all week. The perfect prank that seemed like an accident to get me fired. I don't understand why he stood so close, though. Maybe he wanted to seem innocent, or didn't expect the water to spray as aggressively as it did. Once it started it was like a dam broke.

Either way, Vlad is always setting me up, and I'm confident he's the culprit behind this.

Once we're seated, Marc launches straight into it. "I'm sorry about all that. The dispenser must be a faulty piece of equipment. I'll call the company to have it replaced. Why don't you two start the weekend early? I don't want you to work the rest of the day in wet clothes."

My mouth drops open in utter bewilderment. We aren't getting fired? Maybe this wasn't a Vlad prank, after all. That or he didn't anticipate how compassionate Marc is towards his staff, so his plan backfired.

Vlad replies while I'm still reeling from the past five minutes. "Thank you, sir. See you Monday." He gets up and leaves the office, while I remain frozen in place.

Gathering my wits, I mumble my own quick "thank you" before bolting out. Without lifting my head to look at my coworkers, I grab my purse and exit the building. I'm embarrassed, but at least I wasn't fired.

8

THE PARTNERSHIP

Mirabella

W hen Monday rolls around, I wake up feeling well rested. I stay in bed a few minutes, stretching like a cat before glancing around my room. I'm surprised I woke before my alarm, after such a late-night.

Sylvia didn't get home from her Alaskan family vacation until after Sunday dinner, and we stayed awake well past midnight talking on the phone. I told her about my first week as an intern, including the recent water dispenser incident. Then, Sylvia ranted about her hippie parents and the wilderness trip they forced on her and her brothers. They'd spent the entire week living off the wilderness without even running water as a commodity.

She had a lot to complain about.

Partway through our conversation, I realized I was

still wearing the sweatshirt Marc lent me on Friday. I'd honestly been wearing it almost all weekend, only removing it to paint. In my studio, I lovingly folded it, carefully placing it on one of the chairs, not letting it out of my sight, but also not wanting to damage it.

Vlad didn't utter a word about my clothing choice during Sunday dinner, which was a pleasant surprise. It would've been easy to alert my parents I'd been wearing my new boss's sweatshirt all weekend, but he merely raised a brow at me, keeping his comments and his dinner to himself. The clothing choice had nothing to do with Marc, at least not exactly.

His sweatshirt just smells so good and it's so comfortable. I wish it were mine.

During my phone call with Sylvia, I finally relented. I put it in the washer, in preparation of returning it first thing Monday. I waited to crawl into the bed until after it was clean, dry, and folded neatly on my desk, ready for work.

Forcing Marc to ask me for the sweatshirt would remind everyone of the incident, which I want to avoid. Even if it meant staying up extra late to finish drying the thing.

Dragging my thoughts back to the present, I pluck my phone off the nightstand to scroll through LifeN-ovel, the social media site where everyone shares pictures and posts about their lives. Bracing my back against my headboard, I click on my screen and release a gasp. My fingers immediately relax their hold, causing my phone to drop onto my hip bone when I catch sight of the time.

No, no, no, no.

No way.

I set six alarms.

Today is my sixth day and I'm going to be late.

Again!

No wonder I feel so well-rested. I should've been at work over thirty minutes ago.

All last week my alarms didn't work. I thought I was losing my mind and forgetting to set them, or my phone was broken. On Thursday I even took a screenshot to confirm I set them. After waking up late, again, I finally relented and set an appointment at the phone store for Saturday morning. Instead of holing up in my studio all weekend, I woke up early. Just to be told nothing was wrong with my phone. The store associate tried to upsell me, but I declined.

As I fly out of bed, ignoring my hip pain and scrambling around in my closet to find something appropriate to wear, I wish I bought a new phone. Donning a dress, I tug my long blonde hair into a braid down my back. I swish around some mouthwash and throw on a pair of low-heeled sandals. At the last second, I remember to grab my purse, tossing Marc's sweater inside. Then I rush out the door to my Prius.

I SCREECH into a parking spot at work, barely waiting for the car to stop before jumping out and dashing across the lot. When I burst through the front door, slightly winded, sixteen pairs of eyes immediately swivel to stare at my disheveled form.

Great.

"Mirabella, so glad you could join us today," Marc announces, sarcasm dripping from each word.

It's clear I interrupted the very end of the morning meeting. The board is full of ideas, with names scribbled next to half. I wish I'd taken a few extra minutes to dress. Then, my tardiness would have been less noticeable.

"Err. Sorry I'm late," I respond quietly. Dropping my bag onto the nearest desk, I glob onto the back half of the circle. Most of the eyes have returned to the front, and Marc finally continues.

"We only have a few assignments left," he states.

Normally the meeting is already over this late in the morning. I wonder if they waited for me to arrive, finally starting when it was clear I would be more than a few minutes late. The thought immediately makes me feel guilty.

I don't get to dwell on it for long, as Marc speaks again, "Where was I before we were interrupted?"

I blush when he pointedly looks in my direction. Thankfully, Glenna garners his attention when she shouts, "Interviews with the football players!"

"Ahh right." Marc glances around the room, then points to Vlad. "You." He looks past Vlad's chair and points at me next. "You shadow him."

I immediately want to protest, why Vlad? It's bad

enough I have to spend my whole summer at the Daily with him, but now I have to work directly beside him?

It feels unfair, but I seal my mouth shut, silencing my protests. It's bad enough I was late, there's no reason to cause more drama by questioning my boss's authority in front of his staff. Steeling my resolve, I decide to talk to Marc, privately, after the meeting. I need to return his sweater, anyway.

I barely pay attention as Marc assigns the last few stories. I tap my foot with impatience as I practice our impending conversation in my head. Once everyone disperses, I attempt to follow him into his office, but I'm forced to pull up short when a broad chest blocks my path. I tilt my neck back to find Vlad staring intently at me.

He's a foot and a half taller than my five-foot frame and I think he enjoys making me feel small, by towering over me whenever possible. That he does this often, combined with the smirk he's wearing, helps confirm my suspicion. Either that or he's smirking because he's blocking my way and sabotaging my attempt to shadow someone else.

"Let's go brainstorm some questions for our interviews, Little Mir." Vlad rumbles in his deep, low voice.

He's basically guaranteeing I have to work with him. Since the staff here is comprised of bloodhounds —able to sniff out dirt immediately—I wordlessly follow Vlad to his desk. I have enough issues with my alarm, I don't want reporters prying into my personal life and the source of the tension between Vlad and I.

Vlad seems unbothered by both my silence and our partnership. He boots up his computer, collecting a pen and a pad of paper, and handing them to me. "Have you ever interviewed before?" Vlad asks while logging in.

I shake my head. This entire thing feels like the beginning of a prank. Vlad is acting like he's being helpful, but he's burned me so many times in the past. I no longer trust him.

We didn't always have issues. Five and a half years ago, Vlad and I were best friends. Our parents were neighbors, and by default we spent all our free time together. Out of the blue, his family sold their five-thousand square foot home next door and moved across the main road to a three-bedroom ranch style home.

The Morts are the only family, in the recorded history of our town, to move from one side to the other. Our parents maintained their friendship, but for some reason, despite our compatible personalities and life-long friendship, Vlad decided to hate me.

Six months prior to his move, Vlad began his transition to awful. It all started with him ditching me to join the football team, then slowly evolved into him becoming a straight up bully. It started slowly with taunts about my height, then quickly escalated to larger pranks like my locker being filled to the brim with garbage.

The only good thing to come out of all the suffering was my art. Losing Vlad encouraged me to enroll in pottery and painting. Or anything to fill the void that slowly grew larger as other students joined in on the torment. My few friends ditched me to avoid the wrath of the cheerleaders, but my painting carried me through. I floated above the rumors and abuse.

Well, mostly.

I'm almost eighteen years old, and I've never been asked on a date because the guys in town have all heard about me from the rumor mill. I've never even been kissed! Our town has two males for every female, so the fact that no one has ever asked me out solidifies my pariah status. I'm used to being a loner. I don't need friends except Sylvia, but it would be nice if kids my age didn't consider me a total freak.

The last thing I wanted after my high school experience was to be stuck with Vlad, but it seems unavoidable.

He's been silent for a few seconds, so I raise my eyes from the paper he provided. He was waiting for me to acknowledge his previous question, or maybe him. Vlad nods, interpreting my lack of response as confirmation I have never interviewed anyone.

Even if I was interested in the school newspaper, kids would've just tormented me endlessly. Starting in middle school, I stopped participating beyond the minimum requirements. I've taken all of my art classes and completed all of my projects at the community center or with a private instructor at my house.

"Okay, so the first important tip is: you're there to listen." Vlad taps the notepad he handed me. "Write these tips down. I'll go over this, then we'll start researching the team to formulate informed questions for our subject."

I jot down '1. Listen' on my notepad.

Vlad nods approvingly, then continues. "You want to ask open-ended questions so you receive the most genuine response. You also want to prepare a variety of questions on different topics and have a few follow-up questions ready too, just in case. But sometimes you have to follow your gut and go off script. If someone gives an unexpected answer, you want to chase that story. That's the good stuff."

Scribbling on the paper, I try to capture everything that Vlad told me in a few words. This is the most he's said to me in one sitting since he moved. His advice is actually helpful and shows how passionate he is about his job.

Growing up, Vlad told everyone he wanted to be a sports reporter. He's always played football and was an incredible athlete, even when we were younger. As much as he loved playing, he loved his team even more and enjoyed delving into people's stories, finding what made them passionate about the game. It's part of what made him a good captain, at least according to my dad. So much has changed since Vlad and I were childhood friends, but clearly his passion for inter-acting with people hasn't.

Vlad continues providing instructions for another twenty minutes, then pulls over his desk phone and punches in a number. "Hey Coach, do you think I could stop by with an intern to interview some of your players? We're writing an article for the Daily."

Although I can only hear one side of the conversation, it's clear the coach has agreed. I listen as Vlad finalizes the details before hanging up. He doesn't immediately turn to me.

Instead, he clicks around on his keyboard, gesturing me forward with his hand. "Have you ever seen football stats before?"

Over his shoulder, I see rows of numbers broken down by player and school. My eyes widen at the massive amount of information visible on his screen and I quietly admit, "I've never seen anything like this."

Vlad nods, then patiently explains how to read the numbers. He points at the screen, allowing me time to jot down snippets as he speaks. Once he finishes, Vlad feeds me a mock question, "What is the most difficult part of the season?"

"Am I supposed to answer that?" I reply.

The corner of Vlad's lips tilt up into a smirk. "No, I want you to think up a series of follow-up questions. Weren't you listening?" Instead of the usual mocking tone he uses, Vlad almost sounds like he's joking.

I'm so startled, I stare at my page blankly, my mind working in overdrive.

Vlad prods my shoulder. "Just humor me for half an hour. Then we can go grab lunch and head to the school. I need a few photos of the field before we talk to the players."

I mull over his words. Now he's suggesting we eat together? It's like we're friends again, almost.

The new dynamic he's fostering today makes me uncomfortable. He's being awfully nice, providing useful information about interviews and now a lunch invite... I need to be careful around this version of Vlad.

It could be a trick.

And if it isn't, nice Vlad may end up being more dangerous than the bully version.

9

THE DINER

Mirabella

I'm contemplating my next move as Vlad and I walk across the parking lot. Do I offer him a ride? Do I get in his car? Where are we going to lunch?

I'm unsure how to act in this new, ambiguous friendship territory with Vlad.

Things are never this awkward with my only other friend, Sylvia. She's the planner. Before we left the building, she would've already decided where we're eating and determined who's driving. Then, relay her plans with precision.

Vlad interrupts my inner monologue and answers my unspoken questions by stopping at his car. He states, "I'll drive us to the Diner."

The Diner is the place kids our age hang out. Or so I've heard. I've never been due to the whole bullied-loner-social-status thing. People go there to see and be seen, and I definitely spent most of my high school years attempting to be invisible. Sylvia and I prefer to go to the movies or order takeout and eat in my studio. You know, places without kids from school.

The thought of going to the Diner for the first time with Vlad sends a cocktail of excitement and fear pumping through my veins.

Vlad pushes open the passenger-side door from inside his car. The edge smacks me in the leg, as I hover outside, brooding, and completely oblivious to his movements.

"Are you coming?" He huffs out impatiently.

I scurry forward, but pause at the last second. "No nude coffee stands this time, right?"

Vlad just scoffs and tugs on my leg, causing me to fall inside ungracefully. I land as a heap on the seat. My knees hit the dash and my head bounces against the middle of the back. A soft, lumpy object is pressing into my hip from underneath.

Scrambling to right myself, I dig my elbows into the door and center console, tugging at the lump on the seat simultaneously. Soft fabric grazes the edge of my fingers before I get a firm grip and yank the material up.

Upon closer inspection, I realize it's Vlad's sweatshirt from his high school football team. The fabric has that perfect fluffy feel of cotton that's been washed enough, but not so often as to become threadbare.

After caressing it for a brief second, I wind my arm

back to toss it in the backseat, but Vlad stops me. "I brought that for you. It seemed like you were experiencing a sweatshirt shortage, yesterday."

Mortification zips through me, causing my cheeks to heat, and I twist my head to the side to hide it. I knew Vlad saw me wearing Marc's sweatshirt, but I didn't think he would bring it up.

After my embarrassment fades, I ponder Vlad's sweatshirt, gently stroking the fabric against my palm. This is weird... What kind of tormentor gives their victim clothes?

I should give it back, right?

The action seems appropriate, but thinking about returning the sweatshirt makes my fingers tighten their hold. Even though it's Vlad's, the fabric is so soft and comforting, I want to keep it.

The car ride passes swiftly, my thoughts of Vlad and his erratic personality keeping me preoccupied as we cruise through town. By the time we arrive at the Diner, and Vlad zips his fancy sports car into a spot, I'm no less confused by his actions.

Vlad is becoming more of a mystery with each passing minute.

Tabling the dilemma, I eye the Diner through the windshield. It looks like a spaceship, with a rounded, chrome front covered in glass windows. My eyes absorb the sight with awe. I didn't realize it would look so magnificently retro and chic, all at once.

I'm really here. At the Diner. With Vlad, no less.

He allows me mere seconds to appreciate this

momentous occasion, then pressures me to get out. "Are you ready or are you waiting for an invitation?" His tone is annoyed.

When I glance in his direction, his door is already open, with one foot resting on the asphalt. Shrugging, I reply, "This is my first time here."

The harsh scowl on Vlad's face softens slightly. "Everyone used to come here after school or practice. Why didn't you?"

Shrugging again, I decide not to answer.

Vlad knows how poorly I was treated in middle school and high school. He was the instigator. Coming here would've just been an open invitation for more bullying, so it can't really be surprising that I avoided this place.

I silently exit the car, trailing behind Vlad into the Diner. My eyes are wide, memorizing each detail to tell Sylvia later. Vlad chats with the hostess as she escorts us to a table, but I tune the pair out, more interested in my surroundings.

My gaze darts from the tabletops made of white, glitter-dotted plastic with a rim of silvery chrome, to the red and white checkered vinyl floor. The walls are bright red and plastered in various ads for events happening around town, both past and present. Almost all the booths are full, some with families, but most with kids our age.

When we reach our table, Vlad and I slide into opposite sides. I accept a sticky menu from the hostess and flip through it with a small grin. This feels like the real high school experience, a bit late, but exciting nonetheless.

A waitress approaches our table, holding a pen and order pad. She's wearing a sky-blue dress with a white half-apron and a name tag that reads "Cindy". I examine her as she walks, my eyes skimming her stark white hair and wrinkled face. Her expression isn't very friendly as she moves our way, but a slight smile crosses her face when our eyes connect.

"What can I get for you, dear?"

"I'll just get a medium bacon cheeseburger, please Cindy." Her smile widens as she jots down my order, and I'm pleased my manners pay off.

Vlad surprisingly waits until she finishes writing, offering a smile as he orders, "I'll take the same, but rare."

My eyes track Cindy's movements as she bustles towards the kitchen. Once she's out of sight, I take in the chaos surrounding us. We're seated in a booth near the front windows, close to the hostess stand. It's not quite a corner booth, but still out of the way and easy to see the rest of the Diner.

On the opposite end, four booths are filled with people that look about our age. Guys and girls hop between the tables, laughing and talking loudly. One of my more aggressive tormentors from high school, Kaylee, is sitting on a guy's lap. Her hair forms a chest-nut-colored barrier which has thankfully kept her from noticing me. Her entire group is caught up in their own world, oblivious to the rest of the Diner and I hope they stay that way.

Vlad interrupts my observations with a question. "If you didn't come here, what did you normally do after school?"

Surprise blooms over Vlad's curiosity. Tamping down the feeling, I tear my gaze from the other diners to focus on him. "Sometimes Sylvia and I would go to the movies, but we mostly stayed at my house. Usually in my studio."

"Oh. Like a dance studio?"

I study him, wondering if he's messing with me, but his expression appears genuine. "No, my art studio... where I paint." I watch his face as pieces click together in his mind. "The painting that I gave your parents' for Christmas was one of mine."

It was an intricate watercolor painting of the forest. The foreground held dirt with a few small shrubs. Towards the middle of the painting one dark, lone wolf sat howling up into the air. The backdrop featured looming fir trees and a gloomy night sky. Pride swells as I recall the piece in my mind.

It was one of the best wolf paintings I've completed.

"We've had dinner together every Sunday for the last five years, and I feel like I barely know you," Vlad whispers.

It's unclear if he meant for me to hear his words, or if he was thinking out loud. I'm saved from formulating a response by Cindy's arrival with our food. She balances our plates on her arm, holding a glass of water in each hand. In an impressive juggling act, she's able to gracefully empty her arms without dropping anything, then wanders away.

The second Vlad's plate hits the table, he digs in with gusto. I briefly watch him inhale food. Then, I raise my burger, intent on taking a slightly smaller bite than Vlad's massive chomps. I pause when a slice of pickle hits the table near my water glass.

Glancing around, I attempt to determine where the slice originated from, but there are no obvious signs. Shrugging, I snag the pickle and place it on the corner of Vlad's plate, assuming it came from his burger, purely from the ferocity he's consuming his meal with.

He mumbles an unintelligible response, which I interpret as a thank you. Without further delay, I hungrily dig into my food. My burger is greasy and delicious.

The Diner is amazing. I want to eat here every day.

I'm halfway finished when an object comes flying through the air in an arc. It catches my attention seconds before it hits the side of my head, then plops onto the table. Confused, I swallow and place my burger on my plate.

With delicate fingers, I pick up the mystery item and identify an onion ring. This isn't from Vlad savagely devouring his food. Neither of us ordered onion rings.

My gaze scans the Diner, attempting to identify the culprit. They aren't hard to find.

As soon as my eyes land on a table nearby, the one

with kids from my high school, the girls giggle and a small barrage of fries hit me in the back. In response, I shrink down into the booth as much as possible. I strive to become a smaller target for the food now steadily streaming in my direction.

Vlad finishes his burger and glances up from his plate to see me cowering. "What are you doing?" He asks in a sharp tone, a scowl marring his handsome face.

I reply without looking up or changing position, "Nothing. Just done eating."

As the words leave my lips, half of a bun comes flying from behind me, smacking the side of my face. It slides down slowly, falling into my lap, and I feel a trail of condiments left in its wake.

Peering up underneath my eyelashes, I glimpse Vlad's face and wish I hadn't. He looks furious. I quickly redirect my gaze downwards, hoping his ire isn't directed at me. This is literally the worst-case scenario of eating here.

Vlad pushes himself off the vinyl seat in the booth and stomps to the table filled with raucous laughter. My eyes widen in shock when his voice carries across the Diner.

Although I'm unable to decipher his exact words, his tone is low and menacing. The threat is apparent from his infliction and murderous expression. At one point he gestures to me, still sitting in our booth, and I quickly face the opposite direction so I'm not caught watching.

Vlad returns and throws himself down into the booth across from me. I cautiously glance up from my lap, noticing the boisterous environment has turned somber. Vlad is fuming and focusing on my plate seems safer than continuing to stare. I push my food around as I search for words to apologize for ruining our lunch.

Before I'm able to speak, water bursts out of the glass in front of me. A light spray of the liquid hits my face and chest, with the rest of the glass' contents coating our table. The paper place mats get soaked and the excess water starts a steady drip to the floor. Someone must've thrown something else causing the mess, even after Vlad went to their table.

Cindy rushes over. "Are you two okay?" She asks as she throws a rag on the mess, trying to sop it up. "Do you need to move tables?"

"No, we're fine. Thank you, Cindy," Vlad replies brusquely.

"Can we leave now?" I ask Vlad in a whisper, after Cindy rushes to grab the mop.

"No," he responds flatly. "We're staying here."

He makes a gesture signifying that I should resume eating. He inhaled his food and his plate is already empty, but mine is still half full. Somehow my burger escaped the water unscathed.

Vlad watches me like a hawk as I eat a few more bites. His intense amber gaze leaving my face periodically to glare at anyone else that even dares to glance at our table.

I force myself to finish a small portion of the remaining food, but an anxious knot has grown into the available space in my stomach and I'm no longer hungry. I shove my plate away and move to stand from the booth. Vlad exits his side at the same time, wrapping an arm around my shoulder, and guiding me to the cash register.

"Keep the change," he instructs as he drops a few bills on the counter, then steers me outside into the cloudy, gray afternoon.

His arm remains wrapped around my shoulder, his long strides synced to my much shorter ones all the way to the passenger side of his sports car. He opens the door for me, finally removing his arm and gesturing for me to get inside.

I clamber into the car, resolute that I will never return to this place.

10

THE INTERVIEW

Mirabella

Vlad is sullen and quiet, causing tension to permeate the car ride to our interview. I already feel awkward in social situations, from a pure lack of experience. The Diner incident is something I'm unequipped to handle, and I have no idea how to soothe Vlad's rage.

Do I apologize? Or would that worsen his mood?

Deciding to remain silent, I grab my phone and huddle in my seat, settling my body in the small nook near the door. I shoot a text to Sylvia asking about her classes, but she doesn't message me back. Keeping my phone in my hands for something to do, I delete old emails and read a news article, waiting until the car stops to put it away.

We're a couple hours early for our interview, so I'm unsure what to expect from the rest of the afternoon.

Before we exit, Vlad grabs a large, black, square-shaped bag that looks like an oversized lunchbox.

He catches me staring and states, "Camera, let's go."

Vlad leads me around the school as he photographs the brick building. Then we wander down to the field and he snaps a few pictures of the players in action from the sidelines. I remain silent, observing him in his element.

"What are these for?" I finally ask, as he adjusts the settings on his fancy looking Nikon.

The camera in Vlad's hands makes a clicking noise, and he answers without looking at me. "The images will accompany our article. Since we're a small paper, we don't have a photographer. I take all my own photos and some photos for other reporters in the office."

He clicks his camera a few more times while I process his words. Vlad is an amateur photographer. Who would've thought?

I continue watching as he fiddles with his camera, this time angling the screen in my direction. "What do you think?"

My eyes flit over the image display, impressed at Vlad's skill. He was able to capture the perfect moment. The quarterback is throwing the football, his fingers still extended into the air, seconds after the ball left their tips. The colors are vibrant, jumping off the screen to catch the viewers' attention.

"It's really good," I reply, working hard to keep my surprise from my tone.

Vlad nods, then flips the camera back to face him. He clicks through the images again, eventually dragging his eyes from the display to meet my gaze. "I think one of these will work, we can grab a seat."

I trail behind him to the bleachers, perching on his left to observe the rest of practice. Tipping forward, I rest my elbows on my knees, pretending to watch the players run the field while my mind works in overdrive. At the Diner, Vlad said he felt like he barely knew me, but now I feel the same way.

Vlad used to fit in a perfect box, my rude, but hot ex-best friend. The guy that traded my friendship for popularity.

Either he's changing, or maybe he wasn't who I thought he was. He's helping me at work, he defended me at the Diner, and now he's asking for my input on his photos... which are really good. Like he's an artist.

The sound of the camera shutter snaps me from my thoughts, and I twist my head to find Vlad's newest subject. He's aiming his camera in my direction. He snaps a few more pictures until I throw my hands over my face and yell, "Stop."

I'm not super upset about the photos, but I'm sure I look like a total wreck. There's probably still food in my hair and on my face from the Diner.

Vlad shrugs and places the camera on the bleachers beside him.

I try to discreetly remove my phone from my pocket. I use the screen to check for any remaining food. Luckily, I appear to be free of Diner debris and I release a small sigh of relief as I return my phone to my pocket. The last thing I need is more embarrassing photos of me posted around town.

When my gaze returns to the field, I find the majority of the football team exiting to the sidelines. They appear to be packing their gear and returning to the locker rooms. Next to me, Vlad rises and descends the bleachers, which I take as my cue to follow him.

I stand awkwardly to the side as he greets a dark-haired man dressed in athletic shorts with a whistle around his neck. They do one of those weird, half hug, half back-clap things that men always do and when they break apart, Vlad faces me. "Coach, this is Mira. Mira, this is Coach Martinson."

Coach nods at me, then gestures to the two sweat-drenched football players, still wearing their padded uniforms off to his left. "This is Tony Martinez and Eric Tor. The pair just graduated and are helping run practice over the summer, to give our newer players some field time. We lost a lot of good guys to graduation this year," he states solemnly. I'm unsure whether it's a joke or if Coach Martinson wishes his seniors had failed a grade to continue playing football for another year or two.

"Nice to meet you," I finally murmur to the group.

I inspect the two players while coach and Vlad exchange a few pleasantries. Tony is the taller of the two with a slightly broader frame. His features are sharp, with a prominent brow, a slightly pointed nose, and hair as dark as night. Eric is a few inches shorter with a long, lean frame. He has the build of a runner with a thin face and reddish brown hair.

"Alright, contact me if you need anything else. I'm gonna head to the locker room before it descends into mayhem," Couch says to Vlad, then promptly strides away.

Once he's out of sight, the four of us stand awkwardly for a second. "Should we—" I begin.

At the same time, Vlad suggests, "Let's go—"

We both laugh, then Vlad clears his throat. "Why don't we sit down?"

After a round of nods, the four of us settle down for our interview. Vlad sits awkwardly close to me on the second bleacher. So close, I feel the heat of his thigh against mine, through the layers of our clothing.

While I dig out my pad of paper to jot down notes, I inch a tiny bit away, attempting to be subtle. On his next exhale, Vlad appears to expand, easily occupying the extra space and resuming the contact of our limbs.

Another attempt yields the same results and I decide to leave it be. I don't want to ruin our interview by making a big deal over Vlad's jeans touching my thigh, so I stay put.

Facing the two footballers, I read the first question that I wrote in my notebook. "Half of last year's team graduated two weeks ago. Do you think the dynamic of the team will change this year with all the new players?"

"Definitely—"

"Not at all, Coach—"

Tony and Eric talk over each other, each answering the question with conflicting responses. When they realize they're both speaking, they pause and glare at each other.

"Why don't we start with Eric then go to Tony for each question?" I suggest.

The boys nod, and Eric begins again. "Coach trains us all the same way. I think the team environment he fosters will remain the same..."

Eric's words fade when I feel Vlad's hand on my lower back, playing with the hem of my shirt. I cut my eyes towards him, but he looks transfixed by Eric's response. Nodding occasionally and jotting notes with his left hand, his eyes never once leave our interviewees. He must not notice what he's doing.

Tuning back into the interview, I'm able to ask two more questions before we're interrupted.

"Vlad!!" His name rings out across the stadium, and within seconds, Marvin and Garth jog into view.

They stop in front of our cluster of four, neither of them breathing heavily, despite the lengthy journey across the field. They address Vlad, ignoring the rest of us. "Hey man, there's an issue back at Community Hall. We've been looking all over for you."

With a shuttered face, Vlad turns to me. "I need you to complete the interview and grab a cab back to the Daily." His tone brokers no argument and without waiting for my response, he jumps up and strides away with his two friends.

My eyes trace their retreat across the football field.

I observe as they bend their heads closer together, creating a spectrum of light to dark with their hair as they exchange information. Vlad is tall and built, but he barely has an inch on his friends who are also both big and burly. Once he's filled in, they break into a jog.

I distractedly muddle my way through the rest of the interview, receiving mixed answers from the two players. They don't seem to agree on anything about the team next year and I wish Vlad had stayed to help me form better follow-up questions.

Once we're finished with the questions I prepared, I stand and shake both of their hands. "It was so nice to meet you. Thank you for taking the time to speak with me."

Descending the bleachers once more, I stroll to the stadium's parking lot. I call for a cab twice, but reach voicemail both times. There's only one taxi service in town, with two taxis that must both be busy.

It's unusual, but not unheard of.

Sighing, I dial both of my parent's phones, but neither answer. As a last resort, I call Sylvia, even though she's in class. She also doesn't answer.

Cursing Vlad for abandoning me, I trudge across the asphalt towards the Daily, resigned to having to walk.

The school is almost exactly halfway between downtown and my house, but it makes the most sense to walk back to work. Not only is my car parked there, but I also left my purse in my desk, not wanting to bring it to the interview. A decision I slightly regret, now that I'm stranded.

I've barely made it to the end of the parking lot when a sleek black car pulls up next to me. The window slides down, revealing the dark, inky hair of one of the football players from my interview. Tony.

He yells through his window, "Hey, do you want a ride?"

I hesitate for a mere second before shrugging and opening the door to hop in. "That would be great, thanks!"

Tony has music on low, filling the silence during the short drive. He parks his car across four spots in front of the Daily, leaving the engine idling. I give him a small smile and prepare to exit when he holds up a hand for me to wait. "Hey, are you free on Friday? I'm having a party; you should swing by."

He's inviting me, a total stranger, to his party?

"Uh, sure, I'd really like that." I reply, attempting to sound casual. Meanwhile, my brain is screaming at me, a party? I've never been invited to a party. I struggle to keep my face neutral when I want to grin like a lunatic.

Tony nods his head. "Cool. You're Vlad's girl, right? I'll just send him my address. I have his number from last year."

His words are like a bucket of icy water dumped over my head, and I sputter to correct him. "I, I'm not. Not his girl. I mean, Vlad and I aren't a thing. We just work together."

Smooth.

I want to facepalm myself.

Tony holds his phone out to me. "Oh, cool, cool. Why don't you input your number and send yourself a text? I'll shoot you my address once I get home."

Accepting his phone, I type in my number, hesitating for a minute before entering my name. I end up putting "Mira Love-the Daily" so he remembers who I am and why I'm in his contact list. Then I text myself his name.

"Thanks," I reply, as I hand it back.

Tony gives a brief nod, and I hesitate a second before pushing open the door and exiting. I face the building, stifling the urge to do a little jig until I hear his car zoom off.

My first party invite!

Allowing my body to flood with the excitement I staved off in the car, I dance up to the doors of the Daily. Swiveling my hips dramatically, I yank open the door, sashaying inside without checking my surroundings.

Mid-gyration, I collide into a warm wall of muscle. Firm hands grab my biceps as I exhale an "oomph" on impact. The hold keeps me from falling to the ground, waiting to release me until I've regained my footing.

Without glancing at my savior, I attempt to determine if my embarrassment will allow me to melt into the floor and out of sight. Before I successfully accomplish becoming a puddle on the floor, Marc's voice drifts down to me. "Mira?"

11

THE PARLOR

Mirabella

S orry Marc," I apologize. My cheeks heat with embarrassment when I follow the lines of his arms to meet his emerald gaze. No better way to make a good impression than by being late every day and plowing down your boss.

That's what everyone says, right?

Marc flashes me a smile and I notice he has perfect teeth. All straight and white, glistening in the light shining outside the Daily. "It's okay, I was just locking up. Did you need something from inside?"

Feeling sheepish for interrupting him as he was leaving, I nod. "Yeah, I actually left my purse in my desk earlier. Do you mind if I grab it? I'll be quick!" I reassure him.

Marc probably has plans for the rest of the night that don't involve staying late at work. I don't want him to think I'll trap him for too much longer, but I do need my car keys.

Marc shrugs. "No problem." He extends an arm to hold the door open for me, then follows closely behind as I hurry to my desk.

I open the drawer holding my stuff and see Marc's sweater straight away. "Oh! I have your sweatshirt." I say, while still digging to gather my belongings.

When I straighten with his sweatshirt clutched in my hand, Marc is playing with one of my pens, twirling it between his fingers like a mini baton. It clatters to the desk when he reaches a hand out towards me, the only noise in the silent and still building. He gently takes the sweatshirt, keeping our eyes locked the entire time.

Feeling awkward, I drop my gaze to the wooden tabletop before me. Marc relents and I hear his footsteps as he walks into his office.

I lift my eyes again, watching him drape the piece of clothing over the back of his chair, wondering if I should wait for him or excuse myself to head home.

Undecided, I fill the silence with a question. "Any big plans for the rest of your night?"

Marc leans his hip against his desk casually and crosses his arms. "Not really, I was thinking about watching a movie at home. Do you have any suggestions?"

I shrug. "A relaxing night at home is always nice. Florence is small, so there isn't a lot of nightlife here. Most people just go to the Parlor for an evening treat."

I pause, then tack on, "That's the ice cream shop downtown."

He straightens and uncrosses his arms, taking a few steps forward. "I haven't been there yet. Why don't you ensure you have all your stuff and I'll take us? My treat."

Without giving the invitation much thought, I lift my purse in the air so he can see it. "Everything's in here. I'm ready."

Marc places a hand on my lower back and steers me to the door. I stand to the side waiting for him to lock up the Daily, suddenly feeling perplexed.

Did I just ask my boss on a date?

And did he accept?

MARC DRIVES us to the Parlor, jogging around the front of his truck to open my door once we arrive. He places his hand on my lower back again, gently guiding me into the shop and towards the displayed ice cream.

When we reach the counter, he quickly engages the unfamiliar girl scooping the ice cream. Marc finally brings the conversation to the treat after exchanging pleasantries. "What flavors do you recommend? I'm new in town and to this ice cream shop."

The girl sweeps her eyes across the flavors and grabs two sample spoons. "This one is a big seller. Chocolate fudge."

The ice cream melts on my tongue, creamy and tasty. Personally, I've always been more of a fruity flavored ice cream girl, so I ask, "Do you have anything fruity?" Dumping my spoon into the jar labeled "dirty spoons" while I wait for my next sample.

"We have strawberry," she says, offering us each a spoon filled with pink ice cream. I consume the sugary cream, but before I make a decision, she's offering another sample. "This one is blueberry." Then, seconds after. "Or we have cherry Garcia."

"Oh, wow," I exclaim, a little overwhelmed. Finishing the sample quickly, I order. "Can I get a small scoop of the cherry?"

Marc steps up behind me, waiting until I get my cone to order. "I will stick with a classic. Can I get a scoop of mint chocolate chip in a cup?"

The girl nods her head and hands his ice cream across the counter within seconds. Together, Marc and I approach the register.

"Will you ring them together?" He asks before we reach it, then hands over a twenty.

Once he collects his change, we exit to the sidewalk outside, settling into one of the bistro tables. It's a warm night and surprisingly not raining. Basically, the perfect evening to enjoy ice cream outdoors.

I eye Marc as he devours his scoop of mint chocolate chip and grimace slightly. He raises a brow at my expression, questioning the look.

With a small scoff I ask, "Who orders minty ice cream? Yuck. It's supposed to be a treat, not taste like toothpaste," I tease, lightly.

Marc just laughs, scooping a little spoonful, and

placing it right on top of my cherry ice cream. "Mmm, minty cherry," he jokes.

I respond with a "Bleh" but lick the ice cream off my cone, anyway. "I heard you telling the girl you were new here... where are you from?"

Marc stabs his spoon into the small bit of ice cream remaining, leaving his hands free while he talks. "I'm from a tiny town in Connecticut, smaller than Florence even. My entire family has lived there for years. I'm one of the few Sieves to break free," he replies, referencing his last name when speaking of his move.

I pause, holding my cone over the table. I'm fascinated that he moved across the country and away from his family. Marc appears a few years older than me, but no older than twenty-five. "What brought you to Florence?"

His eyes take on a faraway look as he recants his story. "I've always wanted to run my own paper. A little less than a year ago, I came across an ad that advertised the sale of the *F.O. Daily*. I bought the paper sight unseen and moved to pursue my dreams. Now, here we are." He shoots me a grin and resumes spooning ice cream into his mouth.

I mull over his words. It's odd to me that an ad for our rather insignificant newspaper would make it all the way to Connecticut, but maybe the old owner was desperate to sell. I spend a few more seconds thinking the idea over, before shoving it aside with a mental shrug.

My eyes drift back to Marc and rove his face as we

eat in comfortable silence. He's quite handsome, with a square jaw, prominent nose, and plush lips. As I take my last bite, he asks, "Finished?" Showing he's as aware of my movements as I am of his.

I nod and watch as he gathers the garbage, dumping it into the bin. With the task completed, he places his hand against my lower back again and guides me to his truck. When we reach the passenger side door he pauses, his emerald gaze searing into mine.

Marc looks like he has a question, opening his mouth, then closing it again. He does this twice more before he asks, "Are you and Vlad a couple... Like are you dating?"

My eyebrows raise in shock. That was literally the last thing I expected and the second time today that someone has made this assumption.

"Me and Vlad? No. Our families know each other... our parents are old friends, but I'm pretty sure Vlad hates me. He used to bully me in high school and now he mostly acts like I don't exist," I reply with complete honesty.

Marc's brow furrows, but he says nothing further. He just reaches across my body and tugs open the door for me. He remains nearby until I'm buckled, then he softly closes the door and rounds the hood to jump inside.

We ride in silence back to the Daily, but it feels natural, like we're becoming friends. The type that doesn't have to fill every moment with words.

Once we park, Marc exits and opens my door again, gathering me into a crushing hug upon my feet touching the ground. I attempt to relax into his hold, but it's kind of uncomfortable. Both the fact that I'm hugging my boss in the middle of the work parking lot, after he just bought me ice cream, and that he immediately gave me a massive shock when he pulled me into his arms. Like his skin was overly charged with static electricity.

This whole night has been odd.

Marc finally steps back, his eyes searching mine for something unknown. "See you tomorrow, Mira. Thanks for going to the Parlor with me."

"Thanks for the ice cream." I reply with a small wave before striding to my car. I buckle and wave again when I see Marc waiting by his truck, watching me leave. He returns the wave with a smile.

As soon as I get home, I plop down on my bed and stare at the ceiling. Today was the weirdest day that I've had in a long time.

My phone shows a missed call from Sylvia, but I'm not ready to call her back yet, even though I haven't talked to her in days. I need some time to process everything that happened before dissecting it with my best friend.

Vlad took me out to lunch and gave me his favorite sweatshirt, which I then left in his car. I interviewed two footballers, then one invited me to a party. And I maybe went on an ice cream date with my boss.

12

THE COMPETITION

Mirabella

The next day, my alarm goes off for the first time since I started at the Daily. Before getting out of bed, I flip my phone around between my hands, open all my apps, and play a snippet of a song. All in an effort to figure out if I did anything different, or maybe it was just a weird fluke.

With a sigh, I force my feet over the side of the bed. I guess I'll never know.

On the bright side, waking up on time allows me to leisurely prepare for the day. I straighten my blonde locks, apply several layers of mascara, and a swipe of lip gloss, then peruse my closet for something to wear.

The Daily is casual dress, but Marc, and a few others often wear business professional. I usually pick a happy medium between the two, feeling the whole "dress for success" vibe. Today I choose a pale pink wrap dress and nude, heeled sandals. The look is feminine, but professional and has me ready to tackle the day.

Skipping downstairs, I drop by the kitchen to grab a banana and a sandwich from the fridge, shoving both into my purse. It's so relaxing and pleasant to not be in a frantic rush during the morning.

Yelling out a quick "goodbye" to anyone listening, I exit the house with a huge grin. Humming a song I heard on the radio yesterday, I hop into my Prius and slowly drive to work, arriving fifteen minutes early.

Vlad is exiting his car as I park, and he hovers nearby while I grab my purse. With a deep breath, I brace myself for an interaction with Vlad the Terrible.

"Sorry I had to bail yesterday," he says in greeting, swarming my car the second the door opens. Holding out his hand, he passes me his sweatshirt, the one I left in his car after he ditched me.

I shrug, surprised by his apology and agreeable demeanor. Wordlessly, I deposit the clothing in my car, then gently shut the door. Eventually I reply, "It's fine. Tony gave me a ride."

Vlad places a hand on my shoulder, using his grip to twirl me around. His expression is furious, a menacing scowl with rage bleeding from his eyes. I swear his palm on my shoulder is shaking with anger. "Stay away from Tony, he's bad news," he grits out.

My grin rapidly transforms into a scowl. So much for a pleasant morning. "Vlad, you don't get to dictate my friendships. Especially after you abandon me without a car!"

He's the rudest and most annoying person on this planet.

Huffing, I stalk inside, leaving him standing in the parking lot. My irritation ebbs when I reach my desk and find a box of chocolate-covered cherries with a folded note. It reads: *Saw these at the store after ice cream and thought of you–M*.

Marc is buying me gifts now? Not that I'm complaining, I love all things cherry, but it is a strange leap from a maybe date to a gift on my desk.

Placing the paper down gently, I tuck my bag into a desk drawer. Glancing up, I catch Marc staring at me through the glass windows of his office. I offer a smile and a wave which he enthusiastically returns.

Out of the corner of my eye, I spot Vlad entering the Daily. He follows the direction of my gaze to find Marc. His scowl deepens further, which I didn't believe was possible, and he slams his chair around before planting himself at his desk.

I don't understand Vlad's moods, but I vow to ignore him as much as possible and focus on work, instead. Hopefully, Marc won't force me to shadow him again.

Marc claps his hands and everyone gathers for the morning meeting. I drag my chair right to the front instead of hanging out in the back of the group, like I do when I'm late.

Unfortunately, Vlad plops a chair right next to mine, then does that thing where he spreads out, so he's completely in my space. I release a resigned sigh, already knowing if I scoot away, he'll just take that space too.

I remain facing forward, ignoring him to pay attention to the meeting. It hasn't started because Marc appears to be too busy eyeing Vlad. Glancing between them, it looks like they're in some sort of staring contest. While my gaze is focused on him, Marc blinks, then looks away.

My eyes shift back to Vlad, in time to see the corner of his lips turn up into a smirk. Marc addresses the group but avoids eye contact with Vlad. He claps his hands together twice and says, "Alright, give me some stories, guys. What's new in Florence?"

Random ideas fly through the room and the ones Marc likes are added to the board. It took me a few days to figure out that Marc stays late each night, to print copies of the paper for distribution the following morning.

Each day he assigns new stories to anyone that's finished their previous one. The staff works Monday through Friday. Except for Marc. He holds the big stories written during the week for the papers he prints by himself for Saturday and Sunday delivery.

It's almost hard to believe Marc is only seven years older than me because his work ethic and passion make him seem older. After his story about moving from Connecticut for his dreams, I have a better understanding of why he dedicates so much time to the Daily's success.

Instead of riding his staff to constantly produce clean edits, Marc completes much of the work himself to meet his high standards. Everyone that works at the Daily enjoys working here, but more specifically, for Marc.

Once the board is full, Marc scribbles names next to assignments. I pay little attention, assuming I'll be with Vlad all this week, similar to the situation with Glenna last week.

Vlad's leg muscles, pressed against my thigh, clench and I glance at him to identify the source of his tension. His eyes are fixated on the whiteboard. I follow his gaze to find my name written next to Marc's covering a story about a huge anonymous donation to the local animal shelter.

Vlad seems disappointed, but I don't share the sentiment. Honestly, I'm relieved. His nasty attitude today would make working with him awful. Plus, I'm excited about the story and hopeful we'll get to hold puppies at the shelter, as research.

I also think it will be interesting to work with Marc.... not because the maybe ice cream date or anything. I want his perspective and expertise to assist me in writing better articles. Working with Vlad yesterday was helpful, so I imagine working with Marc will be even better.

Marc dismisses us from the meeting and everyone scatters. Vlad takes an extra-long time to move his chair, huffing under his breath a few times in the process. I don't bother to engage, just wait for him to leave because he's basically in my lap.

Maybe he was planning to prank me today and Marc ruined his plans. Or maybe he wanted me to write the whole article since he abandoned me during the interview. That reminds me, I should probably give him my notes since we won't be working together today.

Ditching my chair at the front, I pluck my notes off my desk and walk to Vlad. He glares at me, watching my progress across the floor with narrowed eyes.

"What do you need? You're working with Marc today," he bites out once I'm standing beside him.

I proffer my notepad between outstretched hands. "Here's the information from the interview yesterday, in case you need it." He looks at the book but doesn't move to grab it. I tack on, "Sorry I can't help you finish the article."

Vlad offers a curt nod, finally accepting my notes and returning his gaze to his computer. He aggressively shakes the mouse and starts pounding against the keys until the screen lights up. I back away, leaving him to fester in his moodiness, intent on searching for Marc to complete our assignment.

I spot him by the water cooler and confidently stride in his direction. Once I'm within earshot he brushes me off. "Hey Mira, we'll go to the animal shelter after lunch. I have a few things to handle this morning, if you could sit with Glenna while I sort them out."

"You got it, boss," I respond, tamping down my disappointment.

Grabbing a cup for water, I watch Marc as he shuts himself in his office. Through the glass I see him logging into his computer, already on to the next task. With a small sigh, I leave the cooler.

Marc and Vlad are both acting super weird, hopefully Glenna is in a normal mood today.

She's quick to drag her chair away from her desk and pull out a magazine once she sees me approach. "Just do the same thing as last week, honey," she instructs, her attention already focused on the pages in her lap.

The rest of the morning drags by slowly as I read articles, keeping half of my attention at the front. Marc barely leaves his office.

After lunch, he finally approaches me at Glenna's desk. "Hey Mira, we need to wait until tomorrow for the animal shelter. Something came up."

I stop typing to eye his unreadable expression. "Is everything okay?"

Marc nods distractedly, but he ends up leaving the Daily shortly after. One eye remains on the door while typing up my story, hoping to see him again, but he doesn't return.

Later, when I'm leaving the Daily, my phone buzzes, shaking my entire purse. I step aside to evade my coworkers heading home and dig through my bag until my fingers touch the slim, metal side. I pull out my phone victoriously, sliding the button across the screen to accept the call.

"Hello," I answer, half-expecting to hear Marc's voice, before recalling he doesn't have my number.

"Oh, my gosh! I've called you three times since yesterday. Why haven't you answered?" Sylvia screeches into my ear.

I wince at the tone and volume of her words, but reply anyway, "Sorry, I got caught up. I have so much to tell you about yesterday." I glance around to ensure my conversation won't be overheard. "Vlad took me to the Diner and I think I went on a date with my boss after work!"

I hold my phone away from my ear as Sylvia shouts random noises until she finally calms down. "I'll be over in a half hour. I need to know everything," she says, then hangs up abruptly.

THE ENTIRE REST of the week, I'm on time for work. The days blur into each other as Marc and I hammer out a few assignments together, including the animal shelter project that he bailed on from Monday.

When I'm not with Marc, I'm shadowing Glenna. She's becoming more and more eager for the knitting expo as it draws near. It literally comes up in every conversation we have. Her articles in the Daily are really ramping up the town too. Everywhere I go, I hear conversations about knitting.

There haven't been any more incidents in the office, but I feel Vlad's glare hit my back every time I enter Marc's office. Marc hasn't brought up our date at the Parlor either, but every day he leaves a box of chocolate-covered cherries on my desk. They're always accompanied by a friendly note complimenting me on something from the day prior. He's very sweet and thoughtful, and it's nice to get little treats. No one has ever done that before.

By the time Friday afternoon rolls around, I'm not sure I'm ready for the weekend. I think I'll miss being at the Daily on Saturday and Sunday. At the end of the day, I pack my bag sadly, looking around the office with morose.

"Hey!" A voice from my left exclaims, startling me, causing me to leap in the air and elbow a cup of water. Marc's quick reflexes save us both from being splattered with the cup's contents. "Sorry, I didn't mean to make you jump," he says with a chuckle. "I was wondering if you wanted to grab dinner tonight."

Facing Marc, I adopt a regretful expression. "I actually have plans for tonight... and for tomorrow. Would you want to do something Sunday?"

As promised, Tony texted me the address for his party. Plus a few follow-up texts saying he hoped I could make it. I finally confirmed my attendance yesterday and Tony answered with sixteen emoji's, so he must be pretty excited. I would feel terrible cancelling on the plans now.

"Ah, sorry I left my invite to last minute. Dinner

Sunday then?" Marc asks. He's taken a step closer so we're almost touching. My body is consumed by a warm buzzing that I don't understand. It's not like attraction, it feels like I'm standing against a dryer on high as it tumbles clothes around.

I clear my throat. "My parents usually have their friends over Sunday, and we eat dinner together." Pausing for a second, I decide not to overthink it and ask, "Would you like to join us?"

Marc wraps his arms around my waist, pulling me closer and forcing me to tip my head backwards to meet his gaze. "Dinner with the parents already?" His tone is low and teasing, and he laughs after he speaks.

I giggle lightly to cover how awkward I feel, then separate from Marc to grab my things. We walk to the exit together, pausing after he locks the door. "See you then?" I ask.

He responds with a nod, squeezing my hand gently before we part ways. I feel his eyes on me as I get in my car, but my gaze scans the parking lot instead of looking back.

There are only two other cars remaining, everyone else left for the weekend. One is Marc's truck, and the other is Vlad's sports car. The latter has the engine running, but his windows are tinted so I can't see inside.

I turn my key in the ignition and begin cautiously driving home. When I check my rearview mirror, I spot Vlad leaving as well. His car follows behind mine almost my entire drive. I periodically glance in the rearview mirror, until he finally pulls off onto his side of the Main Road a few seconds before I enter my neighborhood.

Pushing aside Vlad's strange behavior, I exit my car and stride into my house. Crossing the threshold, I start yelling, "I'm home," but swallow my words when my Mom bursts into the room. She's dressed in her gardening clothes and covered in dirt.

"How was your day, sweetie?" She asks, giving me a soft smile.

I shrug, placing my bag on the entryway table to remove my shoes. "It was fine, work was busy."

My mom smiles at me and pats my shoulder. "I'm so proud of you for using your summer to intern. Before you run off, could you do me a favor and buy me some ice cream? All of this gardening has activated my sweet tooth."

My mom usually has our food delivered once a week, but occasionally she'll get a craving for something sweet. Our normal grocery delivery is all super healthy food, mostly meat and veggies, which our chef whips up into delicious meals.

When my mom is needing sugar, she sends me or my dad to go pick it up from the store. She says that including it in our weekly food order sets a dangerous precedent., even though she asks one of us to go to the store, at least once a week, anyway.

Sighing, I yank my shoe back on and ask, "What flavor?"

She grins. "Your choice. Thank you, sweetie."

I nod and stroll back out the door. Returning to my Prius, I cautiously back down our steep driveway before turning my music all the way up. After a few quick turns, I'm on the Main Road, headed to the store.

Halfway there, I spot someone sprinting down the side of the asphalt in the distance. I slow down a bit and quiet my music. Both precautions to help me stay focused and avoid hitting pedestrians.

As I'm passing the runner who has kept up a hard sprint for at least the last three or four minutes, I spot Vlad! He's running hard and fast, but doesn't look like he's even broken a sweat. I contemplate pulling over after I pass, but decide against it. Maybe he'll be able to run off his terrible attitude from this week and there's nothing for us to talk about, anyway.

Glancing in my rearview mirror a couple minutes later, I spot him still sprinting, turning down a dirt path that leads into the woods. I've never really imagined Vlad working out. I guess I just imagined him as naturally muscular and burly. It makes sense with his build, and his past playing football, that he probably spends a ton of time running and lifting.

With one last look, I see a small trail of dirt kicking up from his path, then focus on the road again. He's a fast runner.

13

THE PARTY

Mirabella

I type Tony's address into my GPS, driving slowly as I follow the directions. Loud bass rattles my car before the house is visible. The closer I get, the easier it is to identify the party. People are spilling out onto the front lawn and sidewalk, with cars double parked down the street.

Parking against the curb a block away, I inhale deeply to gather my courage. With determination, I stride confidently to the door. I was invited and I will have fun.

Upon entering, my bravado falters. I waver between continuing into the crowd of strangers and returning home.

Arriving at the party in full swing, the house packed with bodies of drunken teenagers; I regret my decision to come without backup. I tried to convince

Sylvia to attend, so I didn't have to show up alone. Unfortunately, another girl agreed to be her guinea pig for a haircut, but she was only free tonight and Sylvia declined my invitation to complete her homework.

From my spot in the entryway, I look for Tony, or anyone with a familiar face to convince me to stay. I'm three seconds away from leaving when I hear my name. Shortly after, Tony emerges from the crowd, pushing his way forward.

I stay by the door, my eyes skimming over his inky black hair slicked away from his face, and his fit body covered by a letterman's jacket and dark jeans. He waves enthusiastically, either in greeting or to get my attention, as he continues plowing through people to reach me.

While I wait, my eyes survey the room. Choosing an outfit for tonight took almost an hour. I didn't know what to expect, since this is my first party. I eventually settled on a short, sleeveless, black dress that clings to my body. My favorite part of the outfit is the low-cut back, with extra straps crisscrossing my skin to create a more modest appearance.

When I put the dress on, I was feeling grown-up and risqué. Now, looking around, I see most of the girls are wearing tiny shorts paired with even tinier bandeau tops, and my confidence is faltering. I feel overdressed.

Plucking up my courage, I shoot Tony a shy smile and step down the stairs to meet him. Once I reach the bottom, he throws an arm around my shoulders and pulls me tight against his side. Tony isn't quite as tall as Vlad, but my head is still under his shoulder, so he's basically tucked me into his armpit.

Yuck. Why am I thinking about Vlad at my first party? Probably because he's a lot like most armpits. Dark and smelly.

Tony interrupts my thoughts about the similarities between Vlad and under arms. Yelling to be heard over the music pumping from speakers in the living room, he says, "Let's go get a drink, babe!"

I nod, hoping he either sees me or feels the movement against his chest. It's so loud I don't think he could hear me even if I screamed my response.

Tony keeps me wrapped tightly against him as we wander towards the kitchen. Although the house isn't that large, traveling between rooms is an excruciatingly slow task. Our movement is constantly interrupted, as guys yell his name and offer fist bumps or girls approach with seductive looks. I overhear more than one telling Tony to "find them later if he's free" and I've gotten a fair share of dirty looks for being with him.

We finally reach the less crowded and quieter kitchen. I'm about to escape from under Tony's arm, but freeze in place when I spot the back of a head that looks awfully familiar. I don't have to guess their identity, as I'm dragged over by Tony while he shouts, "Vlad, my man! You made it."

Vlad pivots at the sound of his name and starts one of those one-armed bro-hug-pat-things. He freezes in place, his arm extended at an odd angle when his eyes land on me, still pressed into Tony's armpit.

His gaze immediately hardens, and he steps back. "Mira? Do your parents know you're here?"

Tony laughs, apparently unaware of the sudden tension and assuming Vlad's joking. "Probably not, huh Mir? Most parents don't willingly escort their kids to a house party to partake in underage drinking. Glad you could make it though, Vlad, my man."

Without waiting for a reply, Tony steers me away toward a keg. He excuses us by shouting, "I'm gonna grab my girl a drink" over his shoulder.

I swear I hear a muttered "she's not your girl" behind me, but the music and distance make it hard to be sure.

I FINISH two beers Tony secured me from the kitchen keg and feel fantastic. I've never had a beer before tonight. The drink has made me lightheaded and full, but also loosened my limbs, relaxing me. This party is the most fun I've ever had.

Tony knows everyone. Standing with him has exposed me to a constant stream of unfamiliar faces. Tony keeps introducing me, calling me his girl with his arm lightly curled around my waist. I gave up on correcting him a beer ago. Every time I did, he just smiled and ignored me, anyway.

Some girls that approached us were catty, but after grabbing our third beers, Tony relocated us onto the back patio to hang out with his close friends and their girlfriends. Here there's less traffic from party goers, including the rude girls with the angry glares.

Although I'm enjoying my time with Tony, it's becoming hard to focus on the conversation around me. My bladder is beginning to hurt, pulsing with the need to pee. I've been putting it off because I'm not confident I'll make it on my own, but finally decide it's urgent and separate myself from Tony. After a step forward, I stumble, falling backwards into him.

"Will you help me find the bathroom?" I ask, embarrassed, but still giggling.

One of his friend's girlfriends, Anna or Annabelle, chimes in before Tony has a chance to respond, "We can go together!"

We lean against each other as she yells instructions before each turn, navigating us through the house. "I always come here to party and I know where it is," she screeches to be heard over the music. "Left here!"

I nod and aim my body in that direction, but we wind up in the garage. "Err, maybe it was a right there," she mutters. Nodding again, we return to the hallway, finally finding the bathroom after two more wrong turns.

There's a line, of course, so we recline against the wall to wait.

A new pop song comes blaring from the speakers in the living room. Anna/Annabelle jumps up and down, squealing and clapping her hands together. "This is my song! Will you be okay if I leave you here to go dance? I'll come back once it's over," she promises me with pleading eyes.

"Sure," I respond with a laugh. "Hopefully, I'm out before then and I'll come find you instead."

Anna, or maybe Annabelle, rushes off with a quick wave over her shoulder and I stay lounging against the wall, shuffling a few steps each time the line drifts forward. I'm two people from the door when a large form appears beside me, blocking the dim light spilling into the hall from the kitchen. I ignore them, hoping whoever it is gets the hint I'm not interested.

When the person doesn't move, I flick my eyes upwards, irritated that I can't just wait for the bathroom in peace. My irritation increases tenfold at the sight of Vlad's fuming face scowling down at me. I push a breath out between my lips in irritation. He couldn't just see me here and leave me alone, he had to disrupt my first party. Well, I'm not going to let him ruin it.

Attempting a bored tone, I drawl out, "What do you need, Vlad?"

"Are you here with Tony?" He demands, stepping closer. He towers over me, forcing me to tip my neck back to maintain eye contact.

I meet his amber gaze and reply in my haughtiest tone, "I'm here by myself, but Tony invited me. I came to hang out and meet new people, which doesn't include you."

Vlad huffs. "You shouldn't be on this side of town, it isn't safe for you."

I open my mouth to reply, but I'm interrupted by someone hollering from behind me, "Hey, quit holding up the line. Go to the bathroom or move!"

Glancing past Vlad, I see the open door. The bathroom is vacant, and no one remains in front of me. Sidestepping my least favorite person, I enter the small room and slam the door shut in his face, clicking the lock to ensure he can't harass me further.

Once my bladder is empty, I exit and attempt to hunt down Anna/Annabelle, but I can't find her in the sea of writhing bodies occupying the living room. Eventually, I return to the patio, hoping she's there when I arrive. It takes me an extra-long time to stumble in that direction, and I keep getting lost, even though the house doesn't seem that large.

When I finally near my destination, Tony spots me staggering closer and meets me halfway. He tugs me into his side, escorting me to our previous spot. Tony deposits me next to a railing before jogging away. He drags a stool from the high-topped patio table to where I'm posted and pats the top for me to sit down.

I burst into hysterical laughter as I attempt to clamber up. The stool comes up to just under my chest, making it nearly impossible. I lift one knee, balancing it on the top, but fall backwards instead of successfully climbing up.

Tony chuckles, catching me before I hit the ground. "Steady there," he says, holding me under the armpits. He sets me upright, then adjusts his grip, and lifts me onto the stool like a child. Once I'm settled, he stands behind me so I can rest against him.

I look down, placing my feet on the rung for added balance. When my eyes lift, I see through the sliding doors, catching Vlad's hard gaze on the other side. The conversation around me fades as our eyes lock. Vlad's standing in a circle, surrounded by Marvin, and Garth, and a third friend I've never seen before.

The four of them are in the kitchen, nursing red solo cups. He doesn't seem to pay any attention to his friends, instead he's fixated on me. Tony brushes a hand down my arm, and Vlad tightens his grip on his cup, crushing the sides together in his fist.

My Vlad induced trance is broken when Tony leans down, whispering in my ear, "Want to find somewhere private to hang out, Mir?"

Tearing my eyes from the glass, I blink a few times to refocus. Glancing around the patio, I see most of Tony's friends have abandoned us. Only one couple remain, and they're locking lips against one of the pillars of the house.

I'm about to respond when a deep baritone interjects, "Mira, your parents called and they want you home."

I whip my head around quickly, in the voice's direction. The movement causes my stool to tip forward and I fall into a hard set of abs. A pair of hands on my upper arms stops my momentum, preventing me from dropping further, which likely would have ended with my face landing in the crotch of the khakis in front of me.

Taking a second to recover, I will my head to stop spinning, then glance up. Closing my eyes again, I release a low groan. It would be Vlad's face smirking down at me, holding me back from face-planting against the front of his pants.

"I don't think I can drive yet." I mumble to the floor with flushed cheeks.

Vlad helps me back on the stool and scans my face, assessing me. "I'll drive. We have to bring the guys though; we all came together."

I nod in confirmation, and Vlad turns his back to face me. He bends his knees and looks over his shoulder. "Want a piggyback ride to the car?"

I'M TUCKED into the passenger seat of my car, attempting to tame my nausea, while Vlad drives. Marvin, Garth, and Vlad's third friend are crowded into the backseat, grumbling about how tiny it is. Glancing at them through the rearview mirror, I find the entire back window blocked by their hulking forms sitting one atop another. It's difficult to tell where one guy begins and the next one ends. In the dim lighting, it looks like a giant mass of man meat has taken over the back seat.

After a few minutes, when I'm more confident I won't hurl, I finally snark back, "Why didn't you three just take your own car?"

Vlad laughs over my ire directed at his friends, but still responds in their defense, "We took the taxi to the party, so we wouldn't have to drink and drive."

Marvin chimes in, "We didn't know we'd get shoved into the backseat of this clown car to get home."

I twist my head to face him. "Sorry that when I bought my car, I didn't check if three huge-headed men would fit in the backseat together." It's not my best insult, but it's also, surprisingly, not my worst.

Vlad lets out another low chuckle at Marvin's expense. More grumbles come from the backseat, but quieter now, making them harder to hear.

Fiddling with the radio knobs, I find a song I know and blast it through the speakers to drown out their complaints the rest of the ride home. The song ends, and another begins, but I don't notice if it's one I'm familiar with. I'm too preoccupied by my stomach roiling as Vlad takes a few turns at rapid speeds. I keep my eyes down, fixed on my feet, focusing on my breaths.

I sigh in relief when the car finally slows and start to unbuckle. Raising my eyes to the windshield, I halt my movement to open the door. I don't recognize the house in front of us.

"Where are we?" I ask Vlad.

Vlad's unknown friend lifts his hand in the back-seat. "My house. Thanks for the ride, man." Vlad's other two meaty friends also echo their thanks. Then they push and pull at each other to squeeze their way out of the back seat.

We sit in the driveway another minute, with the headlights on. Watching his friends enter the door, giving them one last wave as they step inside. I level a glare at Vlad once they're out of sight. "I thought my parents called and wanted me home."

He shrugs and smirks, his standard facial expression when he's not glaring. "Tony's bad news. I had to get you out of there and driving your car was cheaper than using the Taxi, it's a win for everyone."

"It was not a win for me." I huff out. "I was having fun, and you made me leave my first party for no reason!" My words make me sound like a petulant child, but I can't help it. Vlad is an expert at getting under my skin. "Take me home, Vlad," I demand.

All I want is to shower and crawl into bed. I was feeling great earlier at the party, after drinking the beers from Tony. Now I just feel fuzzy-headed and nauseous.

"I'm going to take you to my house first and grab you some water. You need to sober up a bit before your parents see you."

I make a "humph" noise in response.

Vlad is being unexpectedly responsible, but I'm sure he has ulterior motives. I need to stay on my toes to make sure he doesn't pull a huge prank on me. Like ditch me in the middle of the woods and drive off in my car or something.

My eyes shift from his face to observe the scenery

through the window as we drive. I diligently watch to ensure Vlad actually takes us to his house, like he said he's going to. My eyes grow heavy as I watch the dark trees blur by the window and I close them for just a second.

I STARTLE and shiver as a wave of icy air drifts over my body. The chill is disorienting, having woken me from a deep sleep.

Where am I? Why is it so cold?

I barely have time to open my eyes before I'm scooped up, with an arm under my legs and another behind my back. A small shock goes through my body when bare skin touches mine. Not in a romantic love story way. No, I feel a small electric current course over my body at the contact.

Gazing upwards, my gray eyes connect with Vlad's amber gaze. "Are you kidnapping me?" I slur at him. At this precise moment, I don't recall why I'm with Vlad. He hates me.

I must've said that last part out loud, either that or Vlad can read my mind now. He replies, "I don't hate you. I brought you to my house to sober up after Tony's party." He stops for a minute and shifts my body in his arms.

He redistributes my weight to his left side and I hear him unlocking his front door behind me. Vlad continues in a quiet voice, and I'm unsure if his words are for my sake or his own. "You couldn't go home yet. I saw how much you drank. I don't know how you're so drunk from three beers, but I don't want your parents to be mad. I texted your mom and told her you were staying here."

"Why would you do that?" I wonder aloud, confused. Is Vlad being... nice? "Are you okay? Did you hit your head or something?" I ask, directing my questions at him this time.

Vlad responds with a look I can't discern in my current state. He closes the door behind us and carries me through the house.

I haven't been here before. Honestly, I knew where his house was, sort of, but Vlad and his parents have never invited my family over. The Morts always come to our house for Sunday dinners. It's still a bit mysterious why they suddenly moved across town. I drunkenly make a mental note to snoop around or ask Vlad tomorrow once I've sobered up.

As soon as he stops walking, he releases my legs, allowing my feet to drop to the floor. I guess at some point I lost my shoes because the soft, plush carpet touches my toes upon impact.

Vlad confirms I'm steady on my own before opening a dresser drawer and shuffling through it. He plucks out a long pair of sweatpants and a huge shirt, shoving them towards me. "Bathroom is through the door to the left." He instructs, "Go in there and get changed."

Following his directions, I enter the attached bathroom and attempt to disrobe. Changing clothes while inebriated is easier said than done. I tangle myself in one of the ten straps to my dress, three times, before I'm able to finagle it over my head and off my body.

Once I'm almost naked, I pull the shirt on first, inhaling Vlad's unique scent of ocean water and forest pine as it passes over my face. When it finally settles into place, it's so large it hangs past my knees like a dress. I put on the sweatpants next, but even with the waistband rolled as many times as possible, there's still a few inches of fabric dragging past my toes and pooling on the ground.

Tripping over the bottoms of the sweats twice, I decide they're too dangerous to wear and place the pants and my dress over my arm. When I reenter the room, Vlad isn't around. I eye the area curiously and place the clothes atop the dresser. I stand there for a minute, contemplating my next move.

My gaze drifts to the bed, which looks so warm and inviting. It's king-sized with four plush-looking pillows. I crawl in while I wait for Vlad to reappear and tell me where I'm supposed to sleep. As soon as my head hits the pillows, I fall into a deep slumber filled with vivid dreams.

14

THE BIRTHDAY

Mirabella

I wake slowly, gradually gaining consciousness as I bask in the luxurious warmth and comfort of my bed. Although I slept well, a terrible headache is pounding against my skull and my stomach is roiling.

Attempting to soothe some of my aches, I reach my arms above my head to stretch. The movement rubs my backside against a firm expanse of skin and I immediately freeze. Whatever I wore to sleep is bunched around my middle and the realization that I'm not alone has me hyperaware of every inch of my skin. The last vestiges of sleep flee my mind as I notice a beefy arm wrapped tightly around my waist and a set of muscular thighs trapping my legs.

Angling my head, I'm greeted by Vlad's sleeping face. An errant piece of dark hair is laying across his forehead, and his expression is peaceful as his chest rises and falls with each deep breath. The sight of Vlad's sleeping form is surprisingly reassuring, as I recall memories of him driving me home last night. At least it isn't some random stranger.

The relief is short lived and quickly followed by indecision. Do I try to sneak out? Do I pretend to sleep until he wakes up?

I've never been in a situation like this before, and I'm unsure how to act.

I wish my phone was within reach, so I could text Sylvia for some advice. Like SOS, in bed with the hottie that hates me. We're mostly naked, what should I do?

Who am I kidding? She would lose her mind and be the least helpful person on planet earth. She'd probably have one of her hmm moments and tell me no better time than the present to lose my virginity or something.

I'm so lost in thought; I don't notice the change in Vlad's breathing right away. It isn't until his fingers start tracing designs on my belly, causing my muscles to twinge, that I realize he's awake. A small giggle escapes my lips when his roaming fingers hit a ticklish spot.

As if startled by the noise, he pauses briefly. I expect him to shove me away and brace myself for the impact. Instead, he tugs me closer, nestling his face into the crook of my neck and inhaling deeply.

My body is stiff as a board, while I attempt to make

sense of this new dynamic. First Vlad was nice and now we're... cuddling? What if this is the beginning of a cruel prank?

Shifting slightly, I crane my neck to make eye contact, so we can have an honest discussion about how he's treated me since he moved.

Vlad grunts, squeezing me tighter, force-stopping my wriggling. "Stop squirming, Little Mir," he grumbles. His tone, and tight grip, make me freeze. He sounds pained and I assume he wants more sleep instead of having to wrestle me.

Deciding it'll be okay to trust Vlad, just this once, I lay my head back on the pillow and close my eyes, but my thoughts continue to run wild.

"I hear your brain overthinking this, Little Mir. Just go back to sleep," Vlad growls.

His words are the last thing I remember before I pass out again.

WHEN I REOPEN MY EYES, I'm lying in bed by myself. I feel substantially more human than earlier this morning. My headache is still throbbing against my skull persistently, but it's not pulsing with as much urgency as it was before.

This time, I stretch out fully, waiting until I finish to eye my surroundings. The room is simple. The only furnishings besides the bed are a single nightstand with a lamp, a desk, and a dark, wooden dresser. A few football trophies are scattered across the desk behind a laptop. The only other personal touch in the room is the painting of a wolf hanging above the dresser.

My feet carry me towards it of their own volition, wanting to get as close as possible to the beautiful piece. It's a lone wolf, with black fur and amber eyes, standing in the snow. He looks hauntingly familiar, as if I've painted this same specimen before, but this painting isn't one of mine.

I step back and inhale deeply as I try to determine my next move. I'm momentarily distracted by the scents of pine and ocean water assaulting my nostrils. Its Vlad's signature scent permeating the air throughout the room. With another deep inhale, I walk towards the attached bathroom. Barely resisting the urge to snoop through his dresser and nightstand as I snag the sweatpants, he offered me yesterday.

After handling my business, I check my appearance in the mirror above the sink. The reflection that greets me is not a pretty sight. My long, blond locks lay across my back in a tangled heap, and the mascara I applied before the party is smeared across my cheeks and forehead.

I twist the sink knobs to high, borrowing a towel to scrub off the dark slashes of smudged makeup. By the time I finish, my face is pink and splotchy, but it's better than looking like I smeared mud all over my skin. I delay looking for Vlad a few more seconds, by running my fingers through strands of my hair, taming them enough to throw into a high ponytail.

Heading into the hall, I feel more presentable, but

not by much. Padding across the soft carpet, I'm forced to hold on to the band of the sweats and raise each foot higher than usual to avoid tripping on the long ends. The closer I get to the kitchen, the stronger the smell of breakfast becomes. Once I identify bacon, I hurry my pace, barely avoiding falling on my face the second before I spot Vlad.

He's standing in front of the stove, shirtless, wearing a pair of sweatpants paired with a hot pink apron. Vlad mans the pans spread on the stovetop like a professional chef, flipping and scraping with fluidity. He must hear me approach, turning in my direction almost immediately following my arrival.

Vlad grabs a glass off the counter next to him, sliding to the countertop near me to slam it down, then rushing back to the stove. I drag my eyes away from his toned back to sniff the contents of the glass. The smell and sight of the oozy, yellow mixture cause me to wrinkle my nose. Even thinking about drinking the contents makes my stomach churn.

Pushing the glass away, I perch on a barstool, using the bottom rung to help me climb atop it. Vlad seems content to cook in silence, but after a few minutes, my curiosity wins out and I ask, "Why did you give me that?"

"It's raw eggs," he responds, not answering my question while pushing some bread down into the toaster.

Yuck.

"Why would I drink that?" I respond, baffled.

"Do you always ask so many questions in the morning, Little Mir? Just drink the damn eggs, they'll help your hangover."

I study his back, hoping to determine if this is a prank or not. His body doesn't give any signs either way. I've never heard of raw eggs as a hangover cure, but I also never drank alcohol prior to yesterday.

Deciding to risk it, I cross my fingers to ward off any potential bad juju from Vlad. I plug my nose with the other hand and chug the slimy liquid down. My eyes squeeze shut as the goop slides down my throat, and when they pop back open, Vlad is standing nearby with another glass. This one contains orange juice, and I gratefully accept it, immediately taking a large gulp and swishing it around my mouth as a cleanse.

By the time the egg taste fades from my mouth, Vlad has served up two plates heaped with bacon, potatoes, toast, and more eggs—cooked this time. Placing one in front of me, he perches on the closest stool.

"Thank you," I say, pleasantly surprised by Vlad's behavior this morning.

He shrugs and grunts, then shovels food into his mouth. I watch for a second, impressed by his voracity, before I dig into my plate.

We finish our mounds of food quickly. Vlad's plate is empty first, but it doesn't take long for mine to follow suit. He hops off his stool and I watch as he rinses off both of our plates, then puts them in the dishwasher.

Instead of immediately turning back in my direction, he takes a few steps closer to the fridge and grabs a small box off the counter. When he faces me again, it's nestled between his palms. He walks closer before placing it on the counter, simultaneously uttering the last words I expect from my hot but rude, ex-best friend, "Happy Birthday Little Mir."

Our gazes collide as I glance up from the box, a sizzling tension immediately sparking through the connection. I rise to my feet, drifting towards Vlad as if carried by a current, unable to fight the pull. I'm steps away from reaching him, our attention solely focused on each other, when the sound of glass crashing to the floor and into a million pieces breaks across the room.

The noise snaps me from my trance and I step backwards as Vlad mutters, "What the hell?"

On the far side of the kitchen, one of the used glasses has broken across the tiled kitchen floor. Vlad mutters something too low for me to hear, wandering towards the pantry to grab a broom. Using his distraction, I sprint from the room, almost tumbling to the ground from the legs of the sweatpants.

I quickly recover and yank open the door to Vlad's bedroom, snatching my clothes from his dresser and rushing outside. Dashing towards my Prius, I hear Vlad call, "Mira," from the doorway behind me. Without stopping, I turn the key in the ignition and drive away like my ass is on fire.

Thoughts war for my attention as I head home. Vlad's behavior the past couple weeks has been odd, especially the connection in the kitchen and the gift.

For the seven-hundredth time during my brief drive, I glance at the seat beside me, eyeing the unopened gift box in disbelief.

It has to be a prank, right?

Indecision fights with hope as I park in my parent's driveway. Maybe Vlad has changed his ways. I waver for half a second before hope wins and I snag the box off the seat to bring inside the house.

When I open the front door, my mom and dad are both waiting for me in the entryway. They yell in unison, "Surprise!" Then swarm me for an awkward cinnamon roll hug, both of them wrapping around each other while they wrap around me. I struggle to return the hug, hold my belongings, and keep Vlad's clothes from falling off my body.

I breathe a sigh of relief when they finally release me, then apologize while slowly inching towards the stairs to change, "Sorry I didn't come home last night."

My dad wraps an arm around my mom and they exchange a glance before their gazes return to mine. My mom smiles, the expression covering her entire face as she responds in a chipper tone, "It's okay, sweetie. Vlad texted us you were staying over last night... we're just so happy you two are getting along again."

Wait, what?

"You're not like mad? That I stayed over at a boy's house..." I ask, perplexed by their reaction.

My dad chuckles, his gray eyes sparkling with mirth. He responds in an equally joy-filled tone, adding to the weirdness of the morning, "Not a boy, kiddo. It's Vlad. We've known him for years and we don't have any concerns about you spending time with the Morts."

"Honestly, we thought the two of you would've become a couple years ago," my mom adds, sighing wistfully. "We had almost given up hope."

This is probably the strangest conversation I've ever had with my parents. Who would be happy that their seventeen, well now eighteen, year old daughter spent the night with a boy? Most kids would have to sneak out to do that.

And with Vlad? He's terrible. He's terrorized me for years. I feel like I've landed in an alternate reality where my parents are encouraging me to hook up with Vlad, and Vlad is being... nice.

I decide not to respond and just nod my head at my parents before I dash up the stairs. Once I'm safely in my room, I lock the door behind me and dial Sylvia.

She answers on the first ring. "You don't think Vlad is suddenly cool, do you?" I shout, maybe a tad aggressively, into my phone.

"Woah. First of all, calm down. Second of all, no. Why the hell would you even have to ask that?" Sylvia replies, sounding surprised.

I exhale a relieved sigh at her response. At least everyone in my life hasn't lost their mind.

Sylvia gives me her undivided attention as I recap the party last night, sleeping at Vlad's house, breakfast, this morning with my parents, everything. I end my story with, "I swear my parents are obsessed with Vlad and blind to the fact that he's a deranged bully!"

When I'm finally done, Sylvia releases a quiet, "hmmm." It comforts me beyond belief that despite all the strangeness from the past few days, Sylvia is still the same person she's always been. I can count on her wisdom in my time of crisis.

"We need to go to the movies, its birthday tradition," she finally says.

Huh.

I was expecting something... different from Sylvia's hmm. Usually she offers a piece of insightful advice I hadn't thought of, not.... this. I allow the silence to linger for a second before deciding she'll have more to say when we meet up.

While on the phone, we scroll through movie listings, settling on a new comedy that shows in two hours.

"I'll pick you up in an hour," I tell her, then we hang up.

At an hour on the dot, I park against the curb outside Sylvia's house. She's waiting for me on her porch, and I immediately notice her shocking and vibrant new hair. It's a bit shorter, but more importantly, it's hot pink.

Rolling down my window, I yell, "You didn't tell me you changed your hair!" She does a quick twirl, then hops into my passenger seat. "You can rock any hair style or color, Sylvia!" I squeal, admiring her beautiful new locks.

"So could you!" She exclaims excitedly. "Ooooh, I know! You should let me dye your hair! Or at least cut it into a new style."

I battle her hands away as she moves to pick up a chunk of my hair for inspection. "No way! I wouldn't look good with colored hair, like you do. And my mom would kill me."

"That's totally not true," Sylvia disagrees, then she adds a hmmm. "Actually, I don't know how your mom would react, but we could always ask her."

Instead of responding, I shake my head and fiddle with the radio. As I pull onto the Main Road, one of her hands strays to my hair again, tugging on a lock. I swat it away with a laugh. "Let me focus on driving."

She nods, picking up her phone to scroll and allowing me to focus. Within minutes, we arrive at the movie theater. Sylvia is bouncing in her seat with excitement, barely giving me time to park before she jumps out of the car and rushes to the ticket window.

By the time I catch up, she's already being handed our tickets and winds her arm through mine to drag me to the concessions. "Ernie," she yells, to garner the attention of the older gentleman working the stand.

"Oh hello, what can I get you two beauties today?" He asks, as he ambles to the counter from the popcorn machine.

"The usual," Sylvia replies simply.

Ernie nods and slowly fills the largest popcorn tub and a giant soda cup with sprite. Sylvia snags a box of M&M's, adding them to the stack of snacks. "That'll be

$15.22," Ernie says, after pressing down the buttons on the ancient register.

I move to grab my wallet, ready to pay since Sylvia bought the tickets, but she stops me with a hand over mine. "Hey, it's your birthday. This is totally my treat."

"It's your birthday?" Ernie asks, before I can protest Sylvia's statement.

"Er, yes," I reply.

Sylvia uses my distraction to slide a twenty across the counter to Ernie. While he makes her change, he adds, "Happy Birthday, Mira. Grab a licorice on the house."

With a genuine smile, I respond, "Thanks Ernie, you're the best."

I grab my pack of licorice, then help Sylvia carry the rest of our snacks to the theater. We're almost fifty minutes early, because I hate missing the previews, but it also means we get to choose any seats in the house.

Settling front and center, Sylvia and I enjoy our version of heaven, eating salty/sweet snacks and watching movie previews in what feels like our own personal theater. Twenty minutes later, raucous laughter trickles in from the hallway and I groan.

Hopefully, they aren't in our theater. I hate when people come to the movies and make noise the entire show; it ruins the experience for everyone else. Movie theaters are the equivalent of sanctuaries or libraries. Silence is requested and appreciated, people.

My annoyance quickly morphs to distress when the group moves into our theater and their faces become visible. It's a group of cheerleaders with their boyfriends. Kaylee and her glossy chestnut hair lead the pack, with her boyfriend Greg at her side. Those two are some of the cruelest people I know.

Sylvia and I exchange a look as they file into the row behind us and she mouths, "Should we go?"

Before I respond, a crinkling noise fills the air. We aren't given time to react. Suddenly slimy objects are cascading onto both of our heads and into our popcorn. I scream in surprise and a piece of something that tastes disgustingly sour falls into my mouth. Jumping up, I spit it out, then wriggle my body to rid myself of anything else remaining. Out of the corner of my eye, I see Sylvia mimicking my movements.

When I look at the seats and the ground surrounding us, I see it's littered with moldy, slimy food, and other garbage I don't want to examine too closely. All the kids in the row behind us are smirking and laughing.

The second my eyes land on her, Kaylee holds up a now empty black garbage bag and says, "Oops."

I stare at the floor as my eyes water, but after a few seconds and a couple deep breaths, I have my emotions under control. I will not cry today. It's my eighteenth birthday. I will not let them make this day about them. Turning on my heel, I stalk into the lobby.

Marching up to the concessions stand, I wait for Ernie's attention. He's preoccupied, so I eventually cup my hands around my mouth to help project my voice across the counter. "Hey Ernie, can I have two garbage bags to cover the seats in my car?"

He turns around from working on the popcorn machine, preparing a new batch of kernels to pop. His eyes widen in shock, his eyebrows raising on his wrinkled forehead as he takes in my messy clothing. Then his gaze drifts to Sylvia standing behind me, also in an equal state of disarray.

"What happened to you two?" he asks gently.

I sigh. "A bunch of kids are throwing garbage in theater three."

Ernie clucks and shakes his head. "I hate when those darned kids do that. Stay here for a minute. I'll grab you some bags and a bin of popcorn to go."

15

THE CURSE

Mirabella

Arriving home from my disastrous birthday outing with Sylvia, I rush to shower before my parents see me. As I traipse up the stairs, I attempt to formulate an excuse that could justify being covered in food remnants, just in case. "I fell in a dumpster" doesn't seem believable, even to my own ears.

Thankfully, I'm able to make it to my room without running into anyone, so I don't have to test it out. I lock the door behind me, waiting to shed my grimy clothes until I reach the bathroom. Cranking the water to hot, I wash away the stench of garbage and linger until my fingers and toes turn pruny.

Leaving the shower, I wrap myself in a fluffy robe and return to my bedroom to towel dry my hair. I'm interrupted by a loud knock on the door. Wrapping up my still dripping locks, I yell, "Come in."

Jacob tentatively pushes his head into my room a smidge. "Miss Love, your mother would like you in her bedroom for a birthday surprise."

I clap my hands together and run to throw open my closet doors. A birthday surprise! What did she get me?

"Thanks Jacob," I throw out as I hear my door clicking closed.

Quickly sifting through my clothes, I find a pair of soft, worn boyfriend jeans and a T-shirt that isn't splattered in paint. I run my brush through my hair a few times so it's not hopelessly tangled later, then rush out of my room and down the hall.

My mom is waiting for me outside her room. When she spots me, a grin covers her heart-shaped face, and she gestures for me to follow her. "I have something to show you, Mira."

I'm giddy, guessing elaborate surprises as my mom leads us to the bookshelf in her room. Pausing, she runs her hand across the bindings before choosing one leather-bound book in the center of the shelf. She removes the tome and I wonder if this is my birthday gift. The idea is quickly dispelled, as the bookcase springs forward from the wall on one side.

Leaping back in surprise, I scream, "We have a secret room behind your bookcase?! How did I not know about this?"

My mom laughs at my reaction, waiting until the last giggle passes her lips before she responds, "Obviously it wouldn't be a secret room if everyone knew about it." She punctuates her sage words by stepping through the open bookcase and onto the stone floor behind it. She stops briefly, looking over her shoulder to address me, "There's more to see, but watch your step, the floor isn't even and I don't want you to get hurt."

Our house is fairly large by any standards. Upstairs, we have six bedrooms, plus my studio and a small den, and then downstairs is a sitting room, a living room, kitchen, and dining room. We also have a small library, my dad's office, and the staff rooms. I'm an only child, but my parents employ a maid, a chef, and a butler. They all live in the bedrooms built off the kitchen. My mom doesn't work, but she stays busy with social engagements and raising me. My father indulges her with the small staff, wanting to make her life easier, and honestly the number of employees my parents have is modest for our side of town.

Even with all the space and amenities in my home, I would never have guessed a secret tunnel existed beyond the bookshelf in my parents' bedroom. Or that it would look like a medieval style dungeon.

My mom grabs a lit torch from a wall sconce, and my thoughts run wild. We have house torches? Isn't it a fire hazard to keep lit torches in a secret hallway? There isn't time to verbalize my questions as my mom quickly disappears from view. I scurry after her, chasing the circle of light bouncing off the stone walls.

I catch up, carefully treading across the stone floor in her footsteps. The hallway winds around twice, angled at a decline. My mom halts abruptly after the second turn, and I'm forced to pull up short to avoid plowing her over. Craning my neck, I see we've reached a steep set of stairs. The entire tunnel has been mostly dark, with a few torches scattered amongst the walls. The bottom of the passageway, wherever it is, has no visible light drifting upwards.

My mom offers me a reassuring smile, saying, "Watch your step." Then she continues forward, descending the stairs.

I hesitate momentarily at the top of the somewhat ominous stairwell. With a deep inhale, I follow cautiously, placing a hand against the cool stone to steady my steps. The light from my mother's torch guides us down the slightly uneven stairs.

A cold breeze flows past my body the same second my foot leaves the last step. I shiver and wrap my arms around myself, trying to hold in my warmth, as I glance around the small circular room. The only thing of interest is a large, wooden door.

My mom removes an ancient-looking metal key from her pocket, inserting it into the lock. As she turns it, a loud, mechanical clicking noise echoes off the stone walls. The door swings open and my mom gestures me forward to enter ahead of her.

I step through the doorway and release a gasp, immediately twirling in a circle, wanting to see everything, all at once. The room is a perfect circle, like the antechamber, with a domed ceiling towering above us. Shelves line the walls haphazardly, some are stacked with books and others hold jars of slime, or colorful looking plants that I've never seen before. One is holding what looks like an orb of blueish-gray light and another holds green smoke. In between the shelves are more sconces with lit torches.

The floor is covered by an ancient-looking, dark-colored rug, threadbare in some places as if it's sat down here for as long as I've been alive. In the center of the room sits a massive table with a large pewter... cauldron.

Is that a cauldron?

A wooden handle is sticking out of it, like some sort of large stirring spoon waiting for use. Next to the cauldron lays another leather-bound book, similar to the one my mom pulled from the bookshelf. This one has been left open, revealing yellowed pages littered with scrawling script.

Looking past the possible cauldron, I notice another table by the far wall containing a stack of knick-knacks. My hands itch to investigate the various items of miscellaneous shapes and sizes.

My gaze continues to drift, spotting a wall with a vast fireplace. A large stack of wood rests on the floor beside it, indicating that it's functional. Two navy-blue armchairs are arranged nearby in a cozy manner with a small end table between.

I wish I brought my phone with me to take photos. Settling for mental snapshots, I attempt to absorb every detail for future painting material. The activity helps to tamper my urge to inspect every object in the room, hoping to learn more about my heritage.

Satisfied with what I've seen, I pivot to face my mom. She's wearing a giant grin, like my reaction was what she'd anticipated. Before I work past my awe, she says, "I'm sure you have many questions. Come sit with me by the fireplace."

I scurry towards the armchairs, eager to learn more. My impatience eats at me, while my mother takes her time to settle in. The second her eyes land on me, I blurt, "What is this place?"

My mom's smile continues to grow, and she replies, "This is our Witching Chamber. We come from a long line of witches, and this room was built over one-hundred years ago by my great-grandparents. To help keep our secret, we constructed our house on top of this chamber, so we can access it at any time, without anyone knowing."

Witches?

"So, is that actually a cauldron?" I exclaim, craning my neck to look at the table behind me.

"Yes, it is. We are potions witches, so all of our magic has to be produced in the cauldron. Some potions require consumption, others can be applied directly to the ground or to another person. Some can even be bottled and released into the air."

I'm mystified.

We're witches? How did I not know?

My parents are incredibly normal, besides the fact

that they love Vlad. I can't believe they've been down here practicing magic and keeping it a secret from me. It almost feels like my mom is playing a trick, but her serious demeanor and the presence of this room lend credibility to her statement.

More questions spill from my lips, "Is dad a witch? Am I a witch? Is everyone in Florence a witch?"

My mom laughs after the barrage, and I enjoy the sound of her lighthearted happiness. "Your dad is a witch, from a witching family. He doesn't practice much though." She pauses, looking contemplative. "You have powerful witching blood running through your veins, but until you join the coven, you won't actually be considered a full witch. It's one of many things you'll learn as you read through our history. You should be a part of an active coven before practicing magic on your own. Besides the simple spells used for training, of course."

Mom gets up and walks to the far wall, brushing her fingers against more books before selecting one. I half expect another wall to open up once it's removed, and I shift to the edge of my seat in anticipation. I'm disappointed when I peek around and realize nothing in the room has changed.

She returns to her chair, perching on the edge before continuing, "About half of the town is comprised of Witches. To live on our side of the Main Road, witching blood has to be present in your veins, although not all witches choose to join the coven anymore."

"Why did you wait so long to tell me?" I ask, processing the overload of information. I'm slightly saddened she didn't want to share this part of her life and our family's legacy, sooner.

"It's tradition in my family to wait until eighteen years of age to reveal our secret. It keeps the information safe and allows you to grow up without magic, which changes your perspective a bit," She admits as she places the book onto the arm of my chair and taps it gently. "This is the history of our coven; you can hang onto it for a while to read. Just don't remove it from the house; we don't want it to get lost out in the real world."

I snag it off the arm, eager to learn everything about magic. I flip through a few pages, stopping when I reach an ancient-looking, sketched image that appears to be a witch casting a spell.

"Can we cast spells?" I ask, holding up the page for my mom to see. So far we've only discussed potions, but maybe that's not all we're capable of.

She looks over the page and her expression morphs into something gloomy. "Many years ago, we were capable of more than we are today. Unfortunately, our ancestors within the coven, and this town, were placed under a curse. Now we can only access potion's magic."

My eyes widen. A curse?

My family is cursed.

I rapidly flip through the book, wondering if it contains the details of the cure. My eyes skim each page, scanning for the word curse. Mom guesses what I'm frantically searching for and puts her hand on top of mine to keep me from thumbing through more pages.

"The book doesn't have any information on the curse. The coven hoped to break it before it affected the next generation and they never added it to our history. I'll tell you more about it later, but how about we head upstairs and eat lunch? This is already a lot to digest for one day, and we have plenty of time for you to learn more."

When I look from the book to meet her gaze, I see a hint of steel glinting back at me. Meaning I should just agree because she's going to force me to leave the room and eat, anyway. "Okay, I guess." I reply reluctantly.

I cradle the massive book to my chest and stand from the armchair. Before we leave the room, I take a few more mental snapshots for future painting material, then follow my mother out into the secret hallway.

Upstairs, we wait for lunch to be served at the dining room table. My mom is thumbing through Better Home and Gardens, and I'm reading the first page of my family's witching history. My thoughts keep drifting to the conversation we had downstairs. Something is poking at my consciousness. As if she said an important tidbit and I need to analyze it more, but I can't figure out what I'm missing.

I flip through a few pages of the book and suddenly a lightbulb goes off. "Hey Mom," I ask, waiting for her full attention. When her vibrant blue eyes connect with mine, I continue, "You said only families with witching blood can live on our side of the Main Road, right?"

"Yes sweetie, it's part of the covenants of the town. The law technically doesn't specify that you have to be a witch. The world at large would lose it if something like that were ever to come to light. Instead, it specifies you must be a descendant of the original families of the coven or in some way related to those families. I don't remember the exact verbiage, but it works on keeping our side witches only." She says with a shrug.

My mind is racing, churning out thoughts almost faster than I can process. "Does Vlad and his family know that we're witches? Why did they move to the other side of town?" I ask, finally feeling like I've caught on to the loose strand of thought from earlier.

Mom's face visibly pales, but she aims a shaky smile at me, regardless. In a flippant tone she replies, "Of course they know we're witches, sweetie. Vlad's parents have witching blood running through their veins too. They lived on this side of town for years."

She pauses and I can tell she's planning a lie or at the very least a half-truth, as she scrunches her forehead searching for an answer to my second question. "You'll have to ask the Morts why they moved across town next time you see them. They probably just wanted a change of scenery." When she finishes speaking, she picks up her magazine and continues to leaf through the pages. Unlike earlier, it doesn't look as if she's paying the articles much attention.

I know she's not telling the truth. My mom doesn't lie often, which is good because she's terrible at it.

Excusing myself from the table, I blurt, "I have something I need to do." Then I rush upstairs before my mom can reply.

When I get to my room, I throw open my closet and shove my coven history book all the way to the back, out of sight. After slamming the doors shut, I snatch up my purse and grab my keys.

Heading down to my car, I yell, "I'll be back later!" Then, I jump into my Prius and cautiously back down our steep driveway.

I have a bone to pick with Vlad Mort.

16

THE DOGHOUSE

Mirabella

I'm fuming as I drive to Vlad's house. The more I think—about the town, our family, and the coven—the more confident I am that the accusation slotting into place, in my mind, is accurate. Somehow, Vlad isn't a witch, which resulted in him moving across town. His parents told him the reason behind their move, and Vlad ruined our friendship because he was jealous. I have witching blood running through my veins and he doesn't.

What a horrible, awful reason to treat someone the way he treated me.

Not only is it out of my control, but I didn't even know. He's tormented me for years, ruined high school, ruined my friendships, and made me feel like garbage... all over something predetermined by genetics?

Well, that all ends today.

I park haphazardly in front of the Mort's, the tail end of my car angled into the street. Rage boils in my blood and instead of correcting it, I stomp to his front porch. I won't be here longer than it takes to yell at Vlad the jealous jerk and move on, anyway.

I'm not sure what I'll say, yet. Honestly, my plan consisted of driving here to scream at him. After that, I'm just gonna wing it.

Stalking up to the door, my anger pulses at the forefront of my mind and I pound my fist against the wood much harder than necessary. As I pull my hand away, the side that hit the door is lightly throbbing. Tucking my hand against my side, I step back and wait for someone to answer. The longer I'm left there, the more my temper flares all over again.

How dare he ignore my knock?!

Just as I raise my hand to slam into the door again, it opens and reveals Vlad's handsome face. His expression transitions from mildly curious to pissed, immediately. His ire confuses me. I'm the only one on this doorstep that has a right to be angry!

Vlad grabs the front of my shirt, using the fabric to tug me inside, and slamming the door behind us. "What are you doing here?" He shouts, his face red and livid.

I brush his hands away, my expression morphing into an irritated frown. "Why are you mad at me? I'm here to pick a bone with you!"

"There's a rabid wolf on the street and it's all over

the news. Why didn't you call? Instead of roaming my neighborhood and putting yourself in danger for no reason," Vlad asks in a loud, exasperated tone.

Oh.

Understanding deflates some of my anger. Vlad isn't mad I'm at his house. He's furious I was lingering outside with an unpredictable, wild animal loose around town. That's actually kind of... sweet.

I glance up, unsure how to reply, and suddenly notice Vlad and I are standing incredibly close. He's currently shirtless, wearing only a pair of basketball shorts, hung low on his hips. I become transfixed by his abs, all eight of them, until his breath draws my focus up to his hard pecs. The rise and fall of his chest with each inhale and exhale entrances me and I'm unable to tear my gaze away.

A loud throat clearing brings me back to the present and I scramble to regain control of the situation. I'm no longer as frustrated as I was before, but Vlad and I still need to talk.

My eyes scan up his broad shoulders, past the amused tilt of his lips, to meet his amber eyes. Our gazes connect and a nameless emotion flares between us right before I dive into the issue at hand. "Have you bullied me for the last three years because I'm a witch and you're not?"

Vlad's eyes widen as his gaze darts around the room. In a low voice he responds, "You can't just shout the word witch wherever you want, whenever you feel like it."

I nod, pretending to understand, then divert back to my question. "Answer me. Is that why?"

Vlad turns on his heel and stalks away. My eyes remain locked on his toned back as he strides down the hall towards his room. With a sigh, I force myself to follow, reaching the door as he sits heavily on the bed, hanging his head. A hank of dark hair flops forward with the movement. He sweeps it away with his hand, but keeps his head lowered.

Hovering in the doorway, I'm not sure what to do. I expected Vlad to deny my accusation outright, then I'd pester him to drag the truth out, but that isn't what's happening at all.

He finally lifts his head, his amber eyes burning as they connect with mine. "I bullied you for a couple months when we were teenagers. After I found out about the curse..." He drops his gaze then continues, "After I found out about the curse, I was pissed and you were an easy target to direct my anger at. You had everything I wanted. So yeah, I guess part of it was because you're a witch. When you didn't react to me ignoring you, I pulled a few pranks, but that's it."

"A couple of months?" I prod, wanting to juice the truth out of him like he's an orange. "You've tormented me directly and indirectly with your followers for years, Vlad."

If he's going to spill secrets, I insist on receiving the whole truth.

Vlad's eyes shoot back up, his gaze is hard, and his jaw set. "I stopped messing with you after I moved.

My parents encouraged me to see the truth... none of this." He gestures around the room. "Is your fault. It's not really anyone's fault. I mean, sometimes at Sunday Dinner, I'll pick on you for your attention, but it's never intentionally malicious. I understand why you stopped being my friend after I left though, no one really has friends from the opposite side of town."

Vlad says the words so convincingly, that I'm confident they're the truth. They seep further into my brain and I slide down the wall behind me, sinking to the floor. Two months. He bullied me for two months. Then stopped.

But no one else did.

All these years, I've ignored Vlad to the furthest extent possible. Until he finally stopped showing up and trying. He probably gave up on me, believing I ended our friendship based on his address. He essentially admitted as much in his heartbroken tone. Meanwhile, I was convinced he was the orchestrator behind all the bullying I was subjected to, both in, and out of school.

"The bullying never ended." I whisper. The tensing of Vlad's shoulders shows he heard my soft-spoken words from across the room. "I thought it was you. Even earlier today, when I had garbage dumped on me. I blamed you. It doesn't matter if you were directly involved... I thought you planned everything with your friends." I stare at my knees during the confession, unable to look at Vlad. My eyes remain fixated, even as

I hear rustling, then his footsteps padding across the soft carpet.

His feet stop directly in front of me, visible through the gap in my knees. I feel too vulnerable to look at him, too raw with the realization that Vlad didn't make these people hate me, or request they treat me poorly. These kids, these bullies, banded together and did it all on their own. Helplessness replaces the space previously occupied by anger.

When Vlad sinks to his haunches in front of me, my gaze remains locked on my knees. I can't meet his eyes. I'd rather sink into the floor, find a new home in the dark space between the carpet and the wooden boards underneath.

It felt different when I was up against one person: a battle of wills, a competition to see who would break first. Me or Vlad. The bullying would end when he tired of his games.

Now, with the words of truth lingering in the air between us, it feels like I'll be on the receiving end of these pranks, for the rest of my life. Will they stop when I'm twenty-five? Thirty? Or maybe never, since there's no clear reason why this all began in the first place.

I feel...weak.

After years of building myself up following the cruelness of others, I believed I developed a thicker skin. One confession from Vlad, one small snippet of truth, and I'm transported back in time to the feelings of despair I had the first time I cleaned used tampons from my locker.

I thought I was stronger than this, but I was wrong.

Vlad places two fingers under my chin, forcing my eyes to his. His face holds an expression of barely contained fury, but to my surprise his words reveal his anger isn't for me. "Who put garbage on you today, Little Mir?" His voice is soft, like liquid honey, stealing my breath with its sweetness that's a direct contradiction to his livid expression.

With a deep inhale, I steel my spine and make the split-second decision to own this new information. The torment is a part of who I am, as much as painting, as much as my parents. It holds no power over me if I own it. I can choose to break, to ignore it, or to fight back.

Before I verbalize my response, a high-pitched animal yelp pierces the air. The noise is close, sounding as if it's coming from behind the house.

Vlad drops my chin and springs to his feet. He's out of the room and down the hall by the time I stagger to mine. I take a single step, shaking out my entire body to regain mobility in my limbs. In my mind, I visualize the movement as a way to shed my helplessness, like removing a knit blanket thrown on for warmth.

With my confidence sliding back into place, I stand to my full height and follow Vlad. He's exiting through the kitchen as my feet hit the carpet in the hall.

"Stay here," he commands over his shoulder as he continues outside.

"What is he doing?" I mutter, hurrying into the kitchen. I push up against the counter to peer through the window into the backyard.

Through the glass panes, Vlad is slowly approaching a massive wolf. Vlad is a giant, but the tallest part of the wolf practically reaches his head. I've never seen an animal this large in the wild. Even standing on four legs, it looks taller than me.

The wolf is baring its teeth, spittle dripping from between his lips and hitting the ground, almost in time with Vlad's steps. Vlad has his hands spread wide in front of him, attempting to non-verbally pacify the beast as he inches closer.

"He's going to get himself killed! He's not even wearing a shirt," I yell into the empty kitchen.

Vlad pauses momentarily, but I don't watch to see his next move. Instead, I scramble around the kitchen, looking for a weapon. There's a distinct lack of wolf-maiming options, so I settle on grabbing the broom. If the wolf lunges, I'll try beating him away with the handle. I justify my decision to leave the house and head into eminent danger, not wanting Vlad completely defenseless against the animal's teeth and claws.

I exit the house, creeping closer to the pair on my tiptoes, and hear Vlad talking in a low, soothing voice to the wolf, still holding his hands in front of him. "It's okay Garth, it's all going to be okay. Calm down buddy, you will be okay."

Garth?

He named the wolf after one of his friends?

My surprise momentarily distracts me, and I forget to watch my step for a half second. That's all it takes for my foot to hit the edge of a rock at the wrong angle and disrupt my balance. Flailing my arms, the broom flies across the clearing as I crash to the ground less than fifteen feet away from Vlad and the wolf.

The yellow eyes of the wolf catch mine, and my heart stutters. The beast emits a deep, menacing growl as his hackles raise. He bends closer to the ground, preparing to lunge, and my life flashes before my eyes.

A series of events follows too quickly for me to completely comprehend. A group of three men, carrying strange looking rifles, burst through the tree line of the woods. They assess the scene, their heads moving from side to side in a sweeping motion. One of them nods and raises his gun, shooting in the wolf's direction, just as his front feet leave the ground, his body aimed in my direction.

Three small darts leave the gun barrel, sailing through the air, connecting with the wolf as his body launches in an arc towards me. The wolf falls to the ground in a heap, less than a foot away. It's the last thing I remember before my vision fades to black.

I WAKE up on my back with a cold, soggy fabric covering my forehead and eyes. I'm groggy and disoriented. Feeling a heavy weight near my feet, my hand pushes against the fabric to uncover my eyes. I find

Vlad sitting on the couch watching TV, as he absently strokes his hand across my ankle.

Memories of the giant wolf and strange men with rifles come flooding back.

"Is the wolf okay? Why did you call it Garth?" I blurt.

Vlad startles, concern evident in his gaze as he scans the length of my body. "Mira!" His voice sounds relieved and his amber eyes soften when they meet mine. "I'm glad you're finally awake." He releases a sigh, "I called your parents and they're on their way to bring you home to rest."

I make a keep-talking motion with my hand, wanting answers to my questions.

Vlad sighs again, this one more resigned than relieved. "The wolf is fine. Animal control tranquilized him, and he's on his way to a nature preserve further away from town. They think he got hungry and wandered here on accident." His eyes turn back to the TV, but he tacks on, "I didn't call him Garth though, I think you imagined that."

I'm about to protest, knowing what I heard, but at that exact moment the front door bursts open and my parents fly into the room.

My mom screams, "MY BABY!" as she sinks to her knees near my face. Her hands poke and prod all over my face and body. "Where are you hurt? Let's take you to the hospital," she says in a concerned tone, while she investigates me.

"Mooom," I whine. "I'm fine. I was just surprised by

a giant wolf and fainted." It's embarrassing enough to swoon; I don't need my parents to make an even bigger deal out of it than it already is. "Can you guys just take me home? I have a bit of a headache, but I think I'll feel better with some sleep."

My dad saves me, swooping in and stilling my mom's inspection. "Come on, sweets. Let's set you up in Mira's car so you can drive it home for her. We'll monitor her at home and if her condition worsens, we'll take her to the doctor."

My mom allows my dad to help her to her feet. Before they exit the house, my dad twists his upper body to address Vlad, "Son, will you load Mira into my car?"

Vlad nods. He pushes my legs off his lap and stands, all in one motion. He lifts me with no warning, placing one arm under my legs and another behind my back, cradling me to his chest with an unreadable expression.

Vlad carries me to my father's SUV like I'm light as a feather, gently placing me into the passenger seat without uttering a word. He doesn't immediately step away, invading my space to buckle my seat belt tightly, instead. To my surprise, he runs a knuckle across my cheek as he retreats, and presses his lips against my forehead in a soft kiss.

As his mouth leaves my skin, he whispers, "See you tomorrow, Little Mir."

The door closes firmly, leaving me in a stunned silence. With eyes wide from shock, I keep my gaze on

Vlad for as long as possible. He stands in front of his house watching the two cars as they pull away.

Even then, he remains on his porch, visible in the side mirror of my dad's SUV. I don't lose sight of him until we turn onto a different street in his neighborhood, headed towards the Main Road to take us home.

This is officially the weirdest birthday I've ever had.

17

THE TENSION

Mirabella

For the first time, I'm eager for Sunday dinner and I would be lying if I said it wasn't partly because of Vlad. Okay, entirely due to Vlad.

Something happened between us yesterday. It felt like a fresh start... and maybe something more.

The look in his eye following our conversation didn't contain the usual annoyance, but rather resembled something closer to affection. Add that to the way he carried me to my dad's car like I was precious cargo... Now thoughts of seeing him don't create the usual ball of dread. Instead, they have my blood thrumming and a swarm of butterflies taking flight in my belly.

My eagerness makes the day feel like an entire week passes in the span of a few scant hours. As I wait out the time before the Mort's arrival, my mind keeps replaying the events from yesterday. Of course, the ones involving Vlad and the mysterious wolf, potentially named Garth. But also, my mom's big revelation.

My family's heritage astounds me, but at the same time, doesn't. It's as if a piece of a puzzle has slid into place, justifying the reason I've always felt different.

I'm a witch. A potion brewing witch.

Part of me wants to rush down the hall into the witching chamber and start throwing objects into the cauldron, but my mom told me to take some time to adjust. Heeding her words, I grab our ancestry anthology and turn to the first page.

A quarter of the way down, my excitement has waned drastically. The book contains in-depth descriptions of bloodlines and the origin of last names, which is dull. So dull, my head begins tipping towards the bed, my eyes drifting shut after twenty minutes.

I'm snapped back into consciousness when my alarm trills, sometime later. Pulling my phone towards me, I stop the noise, grateful I thought ahead and set an alarm to get ready.

Returning the book to its hiding spot, I remain in my closet to get dressed. I change outfits six times, eventually settling on a light blue romper with a flaring, skirt-type bottom that gives the appearance of a dress.

Cute, but casual, I confirm, eyeing my reflection in the mirror.

Normally I don't take this much care dressing for dinner without prodding from my mom, but my mind is urging me to impress Vlad. I want him to notice me tonight.

The thought seems a little odd, so I decide not to dwell on it.

Instead, I continue getting ready. I'm on the last stages of my preparations—flopping my hair back and forth over my shoulders to decide where it looks the best—when I hear the doorbell ring.

"I'll get it!" I yell, flying down the stairs two at a time. When I reach the bottom step, I slow my pace and smooth my hands down my front. Attempting to look casual, I saunter to the door and tug it open.

"Hi..." I say, trailing off when I see Marc, not Vlad standing on my porch. With the events of the past few days, I'd forgotten I sort of invited Marc to Sunday dinner tonight.

Apparently, he did not.

Marc smiles at me, unaware of my inner turmoil as his flawless white teeth glint in the sun. He holds up some flowers clutched in his left hand, adding in a shy, almost embarrassed tone, "I brought you these."

My mom suddenly appears behind me in the doorway in a whirlwind of blond hair. Her blue eyes rake over Marc curiously and she asks, "Mira, who's this young man standing on the porch?"

When I pivot to respond, an amused twinkle in her eye catches my attention. It's a look I don't quite understand, almost like she's teasing me for bringing a boy to Sunday dinner. Ignoring it, I reply, "Mom, this is Marc from the *F.O. Daily*. Marc, this is my Mom, Rebecca."

In the shuffle to shake hands, I'm jostled to the side, maintaining a tight grip on my flowers. My mom notices them and holds out a hand. "I'll take those, we need to put them in a vase so they don't wilt!"

Nodding, I pass her the flowers and my mom scurries away. Her departure leaves Marc and I standing awkwardly in the entry, staring at each other like we've never been on a date before.

For me, that's an accurate statement, but I'm guessing the same isn't true for Marc.

The weird silence lingers for a couple more seconds before I take the initiative. "Would you lik—" I begin.

At the same time, Marc says, "Should we—"

We both stop our sentences simultaneously, gesturing for the other to speak. Our synchronized movements relieve some tension and we both laugh. When my giggles die down, I suggest, "Why don't we wait for everyone else in the sitting room? It's still a little early, so we have some time to kill."

Marc nods and waves his hand. "After you."

I lead him to the sitting room, my family's normal pre-Sunday dinner waiting area. Marc trails behind me silently, his presence keeping me company while his gaze drinks in the artwork my parents have peppered down their hallway. Some from me and some from other artists.

Upon reaching the room, we settle into one of the plush leather sofas, next to each other but not so close we're touching. Spotting a deck of cards on the table, I ask, "Do you know how to play gin rummy?"

Marc nods, following my line of sight. He drags the small coffee table a little closer to our couch and grins. "Game on."

The two of us are amid a cutthroat game when I hear a commotion in the entryway. The doors to the sitting room crash open and Tricia sashays inside. My mother trickles in after her, followed by my dad and Mr. Mort, already deep in conversation.

I try to convince myself I'm not anxious to see Vlad. Yet, when he walks in a minute or two later, my shoulders relax and my eyes drink in his every move. He's wearing a leather jacket paired with dark jeans and the sight of him has a deep exhale leaving my body, ending in a sigh. As if Vlad heard the noise from across the room, his amber eyes lock onto mine, immediately.

We stare at each other until my mother engages him in conversation. They're too far away for me to eavesdrop, so I have to satisfy my curiosity with observing as my mom wildly gestures. Then they both laugh.

A red wall suddenly appears, blocking Vlad from sight. Shaking my head doesn't clear my vision but brings the realization that Tricia's directly in front of me, smiling as she waits for my attention. "Mira, honey, give me a hug! A week is too long to pass without seeing each other."

Returning her smile, I drop my handful of cards onto the table, rise from the couch, and allow her to squeeze the life out of me. She smooshes my face into her bosom, enveloping me into a shockingly tight hold, considering her relatively scrawny arms.

I begin feeling lightheaded from breathing through my flattened nose crushed against her chest. When she finally releases me, I inhale a subtle, deep breath to restore some of the air I lost. After I step back, Tricia focuses on Marc, her eyes flitting down his form now standing next to mine.

He places a palm against my lower back and leans forward to offer Tricia his hand. "Hi, I'm Marc."

"Marc!" Tricia exclaims, "Not the same Marc from the *F.O. Daily*?"

He offers her one of his dazzling smiles. "Yes, that's me."

Tricia's eyes twinkle as she releases her clutch on Marc's hand. "Mirabella and Vlad's boss," she states with a small nod of her head. "I've heard so much, I feel like I know you already. And look at you two, matching for Sunday Dinner!" She gestures at our outfits.

We both glance at each other at the same time. When Marc arrived, I was too distracted by him not being Vlad. I didn't even look at what he was wearing. Then I was so focused on the card game, I didn't bother. Tricia's words, however, cause me to check him out.

My eyes start as his face, zipping over his green

eyes focused on me, down past his square jaw, to finally land on his button-up, the exact same color as my romper. We finish our inspections and our gazes connect simultaneously. Marc's bewildered expression matches my own, and we both burst into laughter.

Instead of a boss and employee, we look like a couple that insists on wearing matching outfits.

My laughter dies in my throat, as my gaze soaks in Marc's handsome, joy-filled face. Ignoring the sudden urge to intertwine my fingers with his, to continue this connection, I face Tricia and reply with a small smile, "Unintentionally."

Jacob saves me from further conversation, striding into the room and announcing, "Dinner is served."

Exhaling deeply, I join the others, filing into the dining room. Somehow, I end up squished between Vlad and Marc, both in line, then at the table.

Both males seem to need more than their portion of allotted space, despite our spacious table. Every time I shift, I bump body parts with one of them, and the smaller I make myself, the more they appear to expand.

Tension radiates as the two guys reach for table rolls at the same time, resulting in a silent stare down over my head. My earlier excitement for dinner is quickly dissipating, and I have a feeling things may end disastrously if Vlad and Marc can't behave more normally.

Tricia interrupts the world's longest staring contest

by engaging Marc in a conversation. "So, Marc, what brought you to Florence?"

I glance at his face, intent on listening to him retell his story about Connecticut and the newspaper ad, but I become distracted. Vlad begins to slowly rub his left foot up and down the back of my calf. It's like a strange version of footsie, and the sensation makes goose flesh appear on my skin.

I'm hyperaware of his movements, watching his face for any sign that his actions are purposeful. His expression doesn't change, and he appears to be listening intently to the conversation between his mother and Marc.

Maybe he thinks my leg is one of the chair legs.

When he finally ceases the motion, I'm unsure whether I'm relieved or disappointed. I try to catch his eye, wanting to mouth a quick "sorry". I feel like I need to apologize for Marc's presence. The sort-of-invite occurred before Vlad and I rekindled our friendship and I'm worried it might ruin everything.

Vlad studiously avoids my eyes, focusing on his food, and the other conversations at the table. Anything that keeps his attention off me. I know he feels my gaze though, because his lips turn up into a slight smirk which he aims at me without looking.

I'm forced to give up, eventually. Marc places his hand on my thigh and I offer him a smile. "Everything okay?" He asks in a low, concerned voice, his brow slightly furrowed.

I answer on autopilot, "Of course, I'm happy you could make it."

Marc offers me another one of his perfect-toothed smiles, then his eyes focus on the other side of me. His grip tightens on my thigh. Seconds later, Vlad starts up again, rubbing his foot against my calf.

I barely resist groaning over both points of contact.

I can't wait for this dinner to be over.

18

THE WOLF

Mirabella

The second the last guest leaves, I close the door and heave a huge sigh of relief. Too exhausted to move, I lounge against the wall and feel the tension slowly draining from my shoulders. That was the strangest dinner ever.

I move to straighten, intending to go upstairs to paint, but the doorbell rings. The chimes echo loudly overhead and halt my movements. Tugging open the door, curiously, I'm surprised to find a bashful-looking Vlad on my porch. He's running a hand through his dark hair, and staring at the ground, not seeming to realize I've opened the door.

"Vlad?" I ask, capturing his attention.

"Uhh hey," he responds, his amber gaze finally locking with mine. "I forgot my coat. Can I come in and grab it?"

It's been unseasonably cold the last few days. Hovering around sixty degrees this week and at night it's even colder, drizzling on and off. It's understandable he wouldn't want to wait until next Sunday to grab his coat.

"Sure," I shrug, opening the door wider to allow him to pass.

Vlad beelines towards the coat closet, shutting it gently once the buttery leather coat is in his hand. He lingers a half second longer, shuffling his feet before he asks, "Do you want to come over? Maybe we could watch a movie and eat some ice cream?"

Pausing briefly, I consider his offer. I was planning to paint tonight. I feel like I've been neglecting my art, now that my schedule is full of work obligations. I miss the peace painting brings. I waver, finally deciding to put it off one more day.

Meeting Vlad's gaze, I reply, "I'd like that. Give me a minute to change."

Instead of waiting for a response, I sprint up the stairs and scurry to my room. In less than sixty seconds, I've changed into a pair of leggings and a drapey sweater. Aiming for comfort-chic, I snag a pair of fur-lined boots, tugging them on as I hop down the hall to rejoin Vlad in the foyer.

His gaze skims over my new outfit, but he remains silent, opening the door and trailing behind me to the driveway. I hover near the side of my Prius, uncertain. "Should we both drive?"

"I don't mind bringing you back later, if you want a ride," Vlad offers.

Nodding, I slide into his smooth leather seat and buckle in. His engine flares to life, punctuating the silence between us with its loud snarl. I tap my fingers on my leg momentarily, then tip forward, reaching for the radio knobs. Apparently, Vlad has the same idea to fill the silence. Our hands knock against each other in midair.

The contact causes a small zap of electricity and I yell, "Ouch."

At the same time Vlad mutters, "You shocked me!"

We exchange a mocking glare, and both chuckle. When our laughter dies off, I reach for the knob again, and this time, Vlad allows me to choose a station. I stop on one playing today's hits, spending my car ride with Vlad listening to pop music.

By the time we arrive at the Mort's, I feel like I'm living in an alternate reality. I'm on my way to watch a movie with Vlad and we're having... fun.

The second we step inside, Tricia wanders out from the kitchen. She shoots Vlad a mischievous look before mock-whispering, "We'll stay in our room, so you two can hang out by yourselves."

I'm not sure if it's intentional, but her words seem to insinuate that Vlad and I are a couple and we need privacy. My cheeks blush hotly in response. Vlad doesn't react in any visible way. He just replies, "Thanks, Mom." And plops down onto the middle couch cushion, picking up the remote, and turning on the TV.

I hover awkwardly until Vlad pats the cushion next to him twice, signaling me to take a seat. I gingerly perch near him, leaving enough space so our legs don't touch. But Vlad seems to expand with each breath, surging closer and filling the distance between us. His eyes are focused on the TV as he flicks through movie options, seemingly unaware of his actions.

Out of the blue, Vlad throws an arm around the back of the couch, curling his hand around my shoulder and tugging me into him. I had been leaning slightly into the arm, to provide him with more space. He had given no indication he noticed, his gaze never leaving the screen.

I learn more about Vlad, each time we hang out together. He's the type of person who notices things, without giving them away. He's constantly observing in silence, storing information for future use.

My body remains stiff under his arm for a second. Then, I allow myself to relax into Vlad, enjoying the warmth and comfort of his body next to mine. Wavering, I finally ask, "Vlad?"

"Mhmm," he responds, his grip squeezing me further into his side, while he clicks the remote with his free hand.

After a deep breath, I blurt, "Marc kind of invited himself to Sunday dinner. I didn't mean for tonight to be weird or anything by having him come."

Vlad's amber gaze slides to mine. He opens his

mouth to reply, and I lean closer, naturally gravitating towards him.

Our lips are centimeters apart, but we're interrupted by a howl. The mournful sound slices through the air. Vlad reacts like the noise was a gunshot, leaping from the couch and sprinting through the kitchen. He flings the backdoor open, causing it to bang against the wall in his haste.

Confused, I follow the same path slowly, careful to watch my step as I pick my way across his backyard. In the faint light from the porch, I feel a wave of déjà vu. A mass of fur is visible beyond the first few trees of the greenbelt.

Vlad is a couple steps ahead of me, but I cautiously pick up my pace to walk beside him. Together, we approach the animal, our steps slowing as we inch closer. The furball becomes distinguishable as another wolf. It's almost as large as the last one, practically the size of a grizzly bear.

Unlike the other wolf, this one is whimpering in pain. His rear left leg is visibly injured, bent at an odd angle, with blood seeping out. The animal appears to have been hit by a car. I step past Vlad towards the wolf, a surge of anger making me bold.

Who would hit this creature? It had to be intentional. There's no way an animal this size wasn't visible on the roadway. Even in the dark, headlights would illuminate something of this proportion with ease.

As I move to pass him, Vlad throws an arm in my path, attempting to form a human barrier to stop me. I push past him, continuing to the wolf. Stopping an arms-length away, I bend down and extend my fingers to their full length, gently stroking the fur covering the wolf's neck.

Vlad grips onto the back of my shirt, like he intends to use the leverage to rip me back. Thankfully, he allows me to continue comforting the poor, majestic creature. He will probably die from someone's negligence, and the thought causes tears to leak from the corners of my eyes.

Sensing my despair, Vlad releases my shirt, intertwining his fingers with mine in a firm, but gentle grip. His palm squeezes mine in silent understanding and support.

Another tiny shock of electricity sizzles between our connected skin, like the spark in the car. My gaze finds Vlad, intent on asking what we can do for this poor animal. Before I'm able to speak, the wolf recaptures my attention. His skin has started vibrating underneath my palm.

My eyebrows raise, but I don't have a chance to choose a reaction. Vlad tugs my hand firmly, propelling my body towards him. He crushes my back to his chest and I feel his body tight with apprehension as the wolf continues to shake.

My confusion amplifies as the wolf slowly shrinks before our eyes, with patches of fur disappearing at a rapid pace. "What?" I gasp out.

Is this some expedited deterioration process? Does this wolf have a disease?

I frantically wipe my hand down my pant leg, regretting the urge to comfort this poor, injured creature. If he was diseased, hopefully it's not passed through skin to skin contact. Or skin to fur contact.

My thoughts are derailed as a popping noise rings out, then suddenly the wolf no longer exists. In its place is a teenage boy, writhing in agony, holding an injured leg with one of his hands. Unlike the wolf's, it's not bent at an odd angle, but it is bleeding.

The boy turns his head and I catch my first glimpse of his face, the low light from the porch glinting off hair that's more red than brown.

This isn't some random stranger lying in the woods. I recognize him.

It's the other guy that we interviewed on the football field with Tony.

What was his name?

Eric.

19

THE COUNCIL

Vlad

Five days ago, Mira saw Eric shift from wolf to human, in the woods just past my house. Apparently, witches don't disclose information about shifters because she did not understand what was happening and fainted almost immediately after.

I think she's officially met some sort of quota for the month. For fainting that is.

After regaining consciousness, she forced me to explain the existence of shifters. The entire time, her gray eyes stared at me with a combination of trepidation and awe. Her voice is forever imprinted on my brain from when she stuttered out, "There are not only witches, but shifters too?!"

The entire situation was uncomfortable. Like giving the birds and the bees talk to an eight-year-old. I proceeded with caution, dancing around the shifters curse until she finally smacked me across the arm and demanded, "Just tell me already. You're being really weird."

So, I told her about the curse on the wolves in our town. About my curse.

If a shifter resists the call of the shift for too long, their mind will deteriorate. As a result, they get stuck as a feral wolf the next time they shift.

The call of the shift happens at inconvenient times and we've all had to learn to keep a cool head even in the most stressful situations. Too much anger, adrenaline, or fear are the quickest way to find yourself with the urge to shift in a less than an ideal situation.

Now, five days following the Eric incident, I'm holding a letter from the Elder Council, addressed to both Mira and I. I flip it between my hands while considering the best course of action.

Maybe it's a thank-you card. Like "thank you for helping a shifter out of a tough situation and comforting him when he was hurt," card. Or maybe it's a personally addressed invitation to the next Shifter formal.

Yeah, fucking right.

Taking a deep breath, I rip off the metaphorical band aid, tearing open the envelope likely containing something sinister. Inside is a single, thick sheet of paper. I unfold it slowly, knowing right away this isn't a thank you or an invitation to wear a penguin suit.

Using my meditative training, I keep my breaths even and tamp down my dread.

I don't have time to shift right now.

Once the paper is unfolded, I read the first five words and skim over the rest before folding it back up. I storm into my house, straight for my room, and yank open my desk drawer. Crumpling the paper further, I shove the request from the Council to the very back. As if placing it so far out of sight could erase it from existence.

If only it worked that way.

The Community Hall has issued a summons for questioning Mira and I. Unfortunately for the Council, I don't plan to tell Mira that she's been summoned. I plan to ignore it.

The summons is more of a threat than a friendly invitation, when all factors are considered.

The Council is vicious, even to their own kind, and they claim the witches are responsible for the wolf's curse. Community Hall is no place for a witch, especially not Mira. They have no authority to enforce their request and I don't want to worry her. Or worse, have her push to see the Council on her own. The last thing I want is to break her trust, but I also can't see her get hurt. It's a fine line, one that I may be crossing, but her safety is my priority.

Shoving away all thoughts of the council, I focus on my plans for the day. I convinced Mira to hang with me in her studio tonight. I've never seen her paint, only recently discovering it's a hobby she picked up after our friendship ended years ago. I'm excited to see her in action. Maybe I can persuade her to paint me.

My thoughts continue to wander, as I sit at the chair behind my desk, fiddling with a pen to release some of my tense energy. In an effort to distract myself from the summons, I throw on a pair of gym shorts and go for a jog.

The second my feet hit the paved road, tension ebbs from my muscles. Exercise of any kind has always been an outlet for the innate anger that comes with being a wolf. When I was younger, my parents didn't understand why I had such a short fuse. I felt like a disappointment for not inheriting their easy-going nature, so I used physical activity to hide how bad it was getting.

Then right before puberty, I started growing faster, my reflexes became unbelievable, my sense of smell was unparalleled, and I could hear anything happening in the house, even a floor away or three rooms over. My parents finally sat me down, six months before they moved us across town. They informed me I was a shifter and they were witches.

A car honking behind me brings me back to the present. My feet carried me to the center of the Main Road, and glancing behind me, I see a trail of cars snailing along, waiting for their opportunity to pass. Waving a hand over my shoulder, I cross to the side and cut through the woods.

Shortly after, I'm jogging through my parent's back-yard and into the house. No one else is home, and I continue my quick pace down the hall to my room. The second I reach my bedroom, I'm flooded with an anxious need to see Mira. Hopping in the shower, I scrub my hands through my hair and slick away my sweat.

Within minutes I'm in my car, fast tracking it to the Love's. My unease lends me a lead foot, and I'm able to make the fourteen-minute drive in less than eight.

Some of my stress drains away as I park in the Love's driveway behind Mira's Prius. Grinning, I snag cupcakes with cherry frosting from the passenger foot well and bound up their front steps. Ready to see Mira, and offer her my gift, I bang my fist against the door, twice. Shortly after the second knock, Jacob opens the door.

"Welcome, Mr. Mort," he says formally, causing my grin to widen in response. "May I take the cupcakes? Mira is in her studio."

"Thanks, Jacob," I reply as he takes the treat for Mira to enjoy later and meanders towards the kitchen.

Watching his retreat for a second longer, I remove my shoes and wander upstairs. I haven't been up here in years, but I plan to snoop around until I find Mira. After checking behind two closed doors that turn out to be guest rooms, I amble towards an open one. Peeking my head around the corner, I spot Mira.

Instead of walking in immediately, I lounge against the door frame to observe her. She's in her element. Wearing a set of headphones and swaying lightly, her brush flies across the canvas. The angle she's standing at allows me to watch as she paints a wolf standing at the edge of a forest.

Tearing my gaze from her dancing form, I inspect the rest of her studio. It's a professional set up, but I wouldn't expect anything else from the Love's. They're the type of family that believes in doing something well or not bothering to do it at all.

I know little about art, so the actual painting supplies in the studio don't hold my interest. What captures my attention is the far wall, entirely covered in wolf paintings. I push myself off the door frame and amble across the room to inspect them closer.

As I pass Mira, I hear her sharp inhale. "Vlad, you startled me. I didn't hear you come in," she says.

I make a mmm-ing noise in response, enraptured by her work. Each painting of a wolf is someone I recognize from my pack, which is strange because I'm sure she'd never seen our wolf forms prior to her birthday. She'd admitted to not knowing about the existence of shifters. Therefore, even if she had seen a wolf from my pack, she wouldn't have known who it was.

My eyes continue examining her paintings. The detail in her art is stunning. It feels like the wolves could run right off the page into this room. I itch to reach out a hand and stroke it across the canvas to feel the downy fur portrayed there.

After a quick perusal, I focus on three paintings centered on the wall. They all feature a dark wolf with amber eyes. My wolf. They're completed with the same level of amazing detail, showing him howling at the moon, overlooking a cliff to the ocean, and in the last one, a small human figure stands next to him, as their backs face the woods.

Mira's voice breaks my concentration. "I actually really need to talk to you, Vlad."

Her worried tone has me pivoting quickly, turning my back to the paintings to address a concerned-looking Mira. "What's going on, Little Mir?"

She's standing near her canvas, her headphones now dangling around the sides of her neck, the paintbrush no longer in sight. As I watch her, she clasps and unclasps her hands in front of her body a few times. Nervous energy radiates off her body in waves.

When she speaks again, my hackles rise. "I received a letter from a Shifter Council. It appears to be some sort of summons. I think I'm in trouble for something and they want to ask me a few questions. Have you heard about this before? Am I not supposed to know about the shifters?"

Her voice started out calm. But by the time she finishes, it's dramatically risen in pitch. Her heartbeat is pounding loudly across the room, punctuating each breath. She's clearly panicking.

I take four long strides across the room and wrap my arms around her tiny body. "Shh, it's okay," I tell her, while silently cursing in my head.

Fuck.

This is why I didn't bring the summons to show her. I can't believe they sent her one too. I didn't think the Shifter Council was allowed to interact with Coven members.

"When did you get your letter?"

Mira's response is muffled by my chest, "Two days ago."

Before I process the information and formulate a plan, a slightly frazzled looking Jacob appears in the doorway to the studio. His chest is heaving, and for the first time—at least that I've ever seen—his tucked shirt is slightly askew.

"Miss Love," he says between two deep breaths. "There are two large men waiting on the porch. They say they're from a Shifter Council and are here to escort you for a summons."

Mira pushes against my body, bracing both hands on my chest as she shoves, hard. I reluctantly release my hold, slowly, looking down at her as I ease her away from my body. Her eyes flit to mine, a flash of fear making an appearance.

She quickly shutters the expression, turning to address Jacob, "We'll be down in a moment to speak with them. Thank you, Jacob."

DUMB AND DUMBER, as I'm referring to them, drive us to Community Hall in a big white van.

They didn't say much at the Love's, other than tell us our presence was required. Mira surveyed them on her porch, taking in their massive forms, before her gaze collided with mine. She said nothing, just briefly scanned my face before she agreed to their request.

As we travel closer to the Shifter Council, I'm practicing some of my meditative breathing techniques and thinking about the upcoming knitting expo. I'm making every attempt to keep my fear and fury under control and prevent an untimely shift.

None of the emotions swirling around my mind are pertaining to myself. I'm concerned for Mira's safety; she is literally on the verge of entering a den of wolves.

The Elder Shifter Council isn't unkind, but they're not known for their compassion. Above all else, their goal is to protect the Shifter Community by enforcing the laws created to do so. If they think our secret is at risk of exposure, they'll stop at nothing to protect it.

The van slows and my attention shifts to Mira, curious what she'll think of Community Hall. Her eyes widen as she regards the sprawling building. She probably didn't even know this place existed. And it's quite the sight to behold.

The outside is reminiscent of a log cabin, made of hulking tree trunks with very few windows smattering the walls. The structure itself is enormous, with a massive, circular main building and two wings stretching off the top in either direction, similar in shape to a crab with raised pincers.

Community Hall is the central location for most aspects of the Shifter Community. Many young wolves experience their initial shift here, myself included. They also hold shifter lessons, provide mentors, and offer a safe haven for wolves in trouble. Once a month, they host a forum to keep the community informed.

A lesser known function of Community Hall is to serve as a jail for shifters that have broken laws, risking exposure of our secret to humans. However, the cells are more commonly used to hold shifters that have lost their humanity to their wolf.

Even as a shifter, Community Hall is intimidating. As we walk up the front steps and enter the large, imposing wooden doors, I try to put myself in Mira's shoes. I imagine what it would feel like to be here for the first time, as a witch, no less.

Dumb and Dumber flank us as we walk, bypassing the smiling receptionist to lead us down the left hallway.

Mira and I continue in silence. I reach for her hand, to comfort her, or maybe myself. The second our skin touches, I feel a small shock, it's like she's constantly covered in a layer of static electricity. Despite that, the touch is soothing.

This entire trip, my overprotective instincts have been working on overdrive. Mira's tiny palm in mine soothes them slightly. I'm still battling with the part of my brain urging me to snatch her up and throw her over my shoulder as I sprint back the way we came. My mind is consumed by thoughts claiming this place is too dangerous for her, urging me to react accordingly.

Instead of forcing her to leave with me, I give Mira's hand two squeezes in quick succession. Reassuring both of us we'll be okay.

To continue distracting myself, I track our path through the building as we wind right, then left, then right again. We're marched down long, windowless hallways lit with fluorescents. I repeat each turn in my mind, creating a long string of directions, just in case. I'm not entirely convinced a hasty exit won't be necessary, in the near future.

Dumb and Dumber finally stop walking once we're deep inside the building, pausing in front of a large set of doors. Dumb gestures for us to open them.

I step forward, tucking Mira behind my back. I use our connected hands as leverage to keep her there, then push the doors open and hope for the best.

20

THE GRANDMA

Mirabella

Tugging on his arm, I force Vlad to let me stand next to him. Instead of cowering behind him as we enter the chamber. His nervousness is rolling off him in waves, and he's barely holding it together. I'm no fragile flower though, and I want to make sure this Council knows it.

Until recently, I wasn't aware the Shifter Community existed. Therefore, a meeting with their Elder Council, or really any interaction within their community, is a new experience for me. I have plenty of experience facing bullies, though. And my past has taught me that things will be worse, if they think I'm too weak to stand on my own two feet and need Vlad to defend me.

He glares at me, but I ignore the look. Instead, I square my shoulders and squeeze his hand reassuringly. I send him some of my mental positivity, my brow furrowing briefly as I project my thoughts at him. We've got this, babe! Wait, err... We've got this, Vlad!

His hand returns the squeeze, tightly, as I observe our surroundings. The room we entered is magnificent. Shaped like an octagon with plush chocolate brown carpet and walls painted a deep, forest green. Like the hallways, the walls are windowless, covered with images of both nature and wolves. Unlike the hallways, the ceiling is covered in huge, oblong sky lights.

Natural light bathes the room and highlights a large rectangular table centered at the front. My gaze drifts over the enormous wooden structure, which is roughly the size of an entire redwood. Behind the slab of unstained wood, four men and one woman observe us silently.

Our audience ranges in age from thirties to early sixties. Despite their young age, it appears this is the Elder Council. Slightly surprised, I inspect them closer, noting their casual appearance, as if they all finished a hike before joining us here.

The eldest looking male, with graying hair and a slightly stooped posture, stands from his seat, garnering my attention. "Miss Love, Mr. Mort, do you know why we have called you here today?"

Without looking at Vlad, I take a half step forward. "No sir, we do not."

Following my words, the Council exchanges glances fraught with unclear meaning. The man and woman closest to the door bend their heads together and conduct a whispered conversation. Vlad's hold tightens, and my fingers lose feeling as his skin vibrates against mine with untamed emotion. I step closer to him, hoping the Council doesn't keep us waiting for long. I'm not sure Vlad can keep it together.

The gray-haired man speaks again, his deep voice booming across the room. "Miss Love, we heard you healed a boy lost to his wolf." My brow furrows in confusion as the man bellows, "Bring him in."

The two guards, which posted themselves at the doorway following our entry, shoot us a look that says, "Don't try to run through this unguarded door like idiots". Then they walk behind the Council's table through a metal door I hadn't previously noticed, briefly disappearing from sight.

I crane my neck, attempting to see where the mystery door leads, but the slight opening reveals nothing. When the guards return, they hold Eric between them. His hands are cuffed, with his head lolling to the side. Most of his weight appears to be supported by the guards, and he barely shuffles his feet to move forward, inching across the floor at a snail's pace.

Placing a hand over my mouth barely stifles the gasp fighting to escape. Vlad tightens his grip on me, tugging my body back as I attempt to rush in Eric's direction. I drag my eyes from his slumped form to catch a warning look flash across Vlad's features. They quickly return to a neutral expression. But his meaning was clear.

Don't react.

The same Councilman demands, "Mr. Tor, repeat what you told us earlier."

Eric's eyes slowly lift from the floor, they're filled with a look of utter defeat. His appearance and expression lead me to believe he's been beaten repeatedly, while in the Council's custody, and he's run out of fight. This guy in front of us is a direct contrast to the confident footballer I met just last week.

I'm surprised when he straightens his spine and begins speaking, "I denied my wolf. It started at football practice. A small fist fight began and my rage skyrocketed, but I didn't shift. Then I went to a party, and my wolf tried to surge free. I resisted until Saturday morning. By the time I shifted, I knew I was in trouble. The second I encouraged it, I lost control. I was all wolf." His words are emotionless, like they have forced him to repeat and perfect this story so many times, the words mean nothing.

As I watch Eric, filled with pity, he attempts to itch his elbow with his leg, like he's still in wolf form. After a few failed attempts, he gives up. My heart aches for this guy who seems to have suffered some unknown trauma and is now being held captive.

Eric's eyes appear sightless as they drift in my direction. They remain aimed at me when he continues, "After chasing a human across the road, a car hit me. My wolf knew we would die from the injuries and limped to the woods, collapsing from loss of blood. I howled as my life ebbed away."

He stops and I squeeze Vlad's hand again, this time comforting myself. Eric looks like he's in some kind of trance. This whole situation doesn't sit right with me, but I don't know what to do.

His voice tears me from my thoughts. "Mira," he says, slowly lifting his cuffed hands and swinging them in my direction. "Triggered my shift. My leg popped into place and most of my skin grew back. Somehow, she saved me, bringing back my humanity!" Each word increases in volume and fervor until he's shrieking. Spittle dribbles down his chin, and his eyes have a crazy glint.

As I watch Eric's hysteria mount, I'm suddenly grateful for the comfort of Vlad's hand in mine. This is the first emotion he's shown, and it's alarming. If the Elder Council didn't frighten me before, they certainly do now.

One of the guards pulls something from his pocket. The flash of a needle glints in the sunlight as the guard jabs Eric, injecting him with a clear liquid. Eric quiets and his body slowly slumps towards the ground. Before he hits the floor, the two guards lift him up, dragging him past the Council and through the doorway.

I bite the inside of my check, to keep my protests inside.

Poor Eric.

Maybe I brought him back from his wolf, although I doubt the truth of that statement. Even if I did, it's clear I didn't save him. Either the Council has caused a mental breakdown, or there was an issue with his shift, but something is very wrong.

After the guards return to their post, the Council-woman rises from her seat, speaking in a firm, crisp tone, "Miss Love, as you can see, you have accomplished something we previously believed impossible. You restored humanity to a shifter, overcoming the urges of his wolf. We would like you to demonstrate this ability again, so we may learn from it."

Vlad speaks before I'm able to, "Eric isn't himself. Even if Mira could 'cure' him as he claims. Aren't you worried about how it affects the shifters, if she's able to do as you say?"

She laughs in response, but the sound is malicious instead of joyful. "Mr. Mort, I think you misinterpreted our request. This is not a favor, it is a command. Miss Love will help the Council. As a witch that is not yet a part of a Coven, I'm sure she appreciates the Elder Council offering friendship, instead of vowing to become her enemy."

Vlad emits a low growl, and I squeeze his hand in a white-knuckle grip. His fear is washing over me in waves, and I'm forced to wade through it as I respond, "When do we start?"

The Elder Council prepared for my immediate acceptance of their task. The guards travel through the wooden door behind the table, this time returning with a gigantic, golden furred wolf. The animal is wearing a metal muzzle, attached to two chains, one clasped in the hands of each guard.

The wolf growls ferociously as he enters the room, and I hear his teeth grinding together behind the muzzle. Even with the restraints, the muscular guards have a hard time controlling him. They're forced to practically fall backwards in order to stop the wolf's momentum as he lunges towards Vlad and I.

At the sight of the massive beast, I'm truly afraid, wishing I could hide behind Vlad. Using all my resolve, I remind myself I'm not that girl and release his hand. Filled with conviction, I steel my spine and approach the wolf cautiously, mimicking the way Vlad approached the wolf in his backyard, with my hands held in front of me.

"Shhh, it's okay," I murmur as I close in on the creature.

His ears perk, and his growling ceases at the sound of my voice. Encouraged, I continue murmuring. Pausing briefly at an arm's length away, I close my eyes and inhale deeply.

A stray thought floats through my mind and I find myself curious about Vlad in his wolf form. Would he shift for me if I asked?

Shaking my head, I reopen my eyes and take the last two steps, bringing my body directly next to the downy fur of the golden wolf. I reach my hand out slowly and gently stroke my palm down his neck. Like I did with Eric.

The wolf leans into my touch and I move a tiny, half step closer. I pet harder, stroking my fingers deep into the beast's fur, scraping the skin beneath with my nails. His eyes flutter shut. The teeth grinding ceases, but his form doesn't shrink, nor does his fur fade like Eric's had.

I meet Vlad's eyes across the room. His face looks bewildered and I'm sure mine does too.

It's as if I've tamed the wolf, but I certainly haven't cured it. Eric was mistaken. I'm not a cure for shifters lost to the curse. Maybe he was more in control than he thought. Maybe he shifted back in the nick of time.

After ten minutes of petting the wolf, I take a step back. He whimpers at me, his green eyes begging for more of my attention. I smile at him, muttering, "I'll see you soon, friend." Not knowing if my words hold any truth, but needing to comfort him before rejoining Vlad.

"Why did you stop?" The female Councilwoman demands.

Exchanging a look with Vlad, I shrug. "When we found Eric, he changed within sixty seconds of me touching his fur. If I could cure this poor shifter, it would've already happened by now," I inform the Council. I make eye contact, one by one, to help drive my point across.

"You're not leaving until you heal one of my shifters!" The Councilwoman shrieks.

At the end of her statement, the bulky wooden doors leading into the room fly open, hitting the wall on either side with a loud bang. The noise causes me to jump slightly, and Vlad pulls me into his chest, offering me his reassurance and protection.

My eyes widen as a petite woman with gray hair and a billowing robe strides into the room. "You should be ashamed of yourselves Council," the woman calls out in a confident, nasally tone as she moves towards Vlad and I. "You know as well as I, that it's against the law to go after a Witch that just turned of age to join her Coven."

The gray-haired man stands from behind the table again. "Ahh, Molly Spells. I would say it's a pleasure to see you again, but I don't like to lie. You're not allowed at Community Hall... after the last incident."

The woman named Molly pulls a scroll from somewhere off her person and rolls it out in front of her. She walks confidently to the Council and slaps it violently onto the table. I barely stifle my laugh as three of the five jump and recoil as if she's just laid a snake or dead rodent in front of them.

Molly scoffs, standing tall and proud before the Council. Her shoulders are back, her hands on her hips, her head held high. These men, and woman, don't seem to frighten her at all. Her attitude gives me courage, causing me to straighten my posture even as I remain pressed against Vlad.

"Oh, come on. It's an immunity scroll, not poison." Molly drawls out. "The Coven has granted me immunity to come and rescue their future apprentice and her boyfriend from your clutches. You have no right to detain them here, or to force my granddaughter to use magic she has no experience, nor business experimenting with, Sylvester." At the end of her statement, she looks directly at the gray-haired man. I'm guessing he's Sylvester, and I'm also guessing there's some history between the two.

The longer I stand there and think about her statement, the more one word pulses to the front of my brain until I acknowledge it.

Granddaughter.

I have a grandmother?

21

THE TRUTH

Mirabella

My newfound grandma exchanges several quips with the Council. Her face eventually pulls into a deep frown and she removes a small, green, circular bottle from within her robes. The Council must be familiar with the contents because their protests immediately stop. And they reluctantly let us leave. As Vlad tugs me towards the door, Sylvester issues a final statement that sounds more like a threat. "Miss Love, Mr. Mort. We'll be monitoring you."

I remember little about leaving after that. My head is filled with thoughts about my grandmother. I've gone eighteen years thinking my grandparents were all dead. Finding out one is alive is a complete shock to my system. More overwhelming than our run-in with the Council, even.

Don't get me wrong, I'm grateful Molly saved us, but also confused. Questions rapidly flood my mind, overshadowing everything else. If she knew I existed, why didn't she find me sooner? Wasn't she curious about me? Didn't she want to watch me grow up?

My stomach churns with anxiety. Over the Council, my grandmother, and the fact that my parents lied to me. Growing up, my mom and dad always said that we're the only family each other has, but that wasn't true.

The second we reach the stairs to Community Hall's parking lot, my legs stop working. I sink down to my haunches as I drown in my thoughts. First witches, then shifters, and now a secret grandma?

It's all too much.

Vlad is the first to notice I'm no longer trailing behind them. He stops mid-stride, with his leg in the air. He twists his head to the side, a look of panic overtaking his face until he spots me hunched over, clutching my stomach. He backtracks three steps, crouching next to me.

"Are you okay?" He asks, his voice low and filled with concern.

"Why did she wait until now?" I ask, mid-thought.

Vlad follows my gaze to my grandma. She's paused a few steps down and appears to have heard my whispered question. A frown crosses her face, but she quickly straightens her expression. "Come along, dears. I'm sure you both have many questions, but this is neither the time nor place. Even the trees have ears around these parts," she mutters, her crystalline-blue eyes, the same color as my mother's, glancing around.

Placing a hand under my elbow, Vlad half-drags me back into a standing position. My grandmother nods approvingly. "Much better. Let's get to my house and you can ask all the questions you'd like, hmm?"

I nod in response, some of my anxious energy ebbing at her words. I have a lot of questions. Vlad twines his hand with mine as we take our first step. He passes on a bit of static electricity, like he always seems to do when our bare skin touches. Maybe it's a shifter thing, and static clings to their fur or something.

My grandma starts chattering again, but adjusts her pace to stay beside us. "Did they let you drive yourselves?"

Vlad and I exchange a glance, shaking our heads in sync.

She releases a deep sigh. "No matter, it's probably easier if I just drive you, anyway. My house can be hard to find the first time." She stops when we reach an ancient-looking Chevelle, gesturing for us to get in.

The three of us pile inside, with Vlad in the passenger seat for the extra bit of space. Even in the front seat, he looks ridiculously huge in the small vehicle. One bump in the road and he might end up taking out the window with his elbow. It lightens my mood to see him crammed up there. A laugh escapes and I belatedly lift a hand to stifle it.

Hearing my giggle, Vlad cranes his neck to see what's happening in the back seat. His stunted movements make me laugh harder at his expense. He's quick to catch on to the reason for my humor, and soon he and my grandmother join in, laughing at the clown car type scenario.

After we collect ourselves, my grandma turns over the ignition and zips away from the building. I watch out the rear window, relieved as Community Hall rapidly fades from view. We remain on Main Road for a couple minutes in companionable silence before turning onto a dirt path that appears on the shifter side.

We drive for miles down that road, which is entirely unpaved, making it a rough journey. The car bounces along at a slow pace, and the forest surrounding us becomes denser, indicating we are getting further from the rest of the town. My grandmother takes a sudden left, past a boulder, onto an even smaller, less-maintained dirt road. We jolt along another five minutes, stopping in front of the most beautiful tree in the entire forest.

It sits, low and squat, maybe five feet off the ground, but sprawling in each direction, out of my line of sight. Even if Vlad's form wasn't blocking half the windshield, I wouldn't be able to see the end of the gigantic piece of nature. As I stare, I realize there's a small, paneled cottage nestled behind the curtain of vibrant, green leaves. It looks like the house that Snow White would live in, placed on a portion of the tree's trunk.

It's stunning.

My grandma shuts off her ancient car, addressing Vlad and I, "This is it. Let's head inside and I'll answer questions."

Together we ascend the few steps into the tree, approaching a red front door. The entire time I crane my neck, wanting to see everything at once. The house is literally settled on top of the branches, snuggled perfectly inside, as if the house came first and the tree grew up around it, holding it between its branches, protecting it from prying eyes with a shield of leaves.

Stepping inside the tree-cottage, I find the interior cluttered and eclectic. The door opens right into a crowded living room, with two floral-patterned couches, a dark wooden coffee table, and a wall entirely filled with books and knick-knacks. A pink chair sits off to one side, with an end table on either side of it, creating a cozy corner. Each of the tables is also piled high with books, scrolls, and papers. An open doorway leads into the next room and I fight the urge to continue exploring, wanting to discover more about my grandma and how she lives.

"Have a seat. I'll go make us some tea, then we'll settle in for a talk," my grandmother instructs before puttering further into her house.

Vlad and I sit on one of the floral couches together, side-by-side. He expands into the space, but for once I allow myself to lean into him, accepting the comfort he offers without words. His arm tugs me into his side and I rest my head against his chest.

Once I'm comfortable, I realize the angle of the couch allows us a glimpse into the kitchen. I unashamedly stare inside the room, examining every visible inch. The floor is covered by beige tile, topped by dark cabinets and colorful countertops. The surfaces discernible from our vantage point appear to be cluttered with kitchen gadgets and more books.

From the little I've seen so far, it wouldn't surprise me to find my grandmother's bed completely covered in books as well. I've never seen so many in one place, except for maybe the Portland Library a few hours away.

Vlad squeezes my leg and I tip my neck back to look at him. He's staring quizzically at the bookshelf across the room and I follow his line of sight. On the shelf, a small figurine of a black cat sits in a stretching pose. My eyes widen when the cat leaves the stretch, moving to pace instead. Weaving between the books and other knick-knacks in a path, the cat steadily paces back and forth.

My grandma's burgundy robe suddenly blocks my view as she bustles into the living room, setting a full tray onto the coffee table. It's laden with a kettle, cups, some biscuits, and a few other odds and ends.

She takes her time, pouring a cup for Vlad and I, then claiming one for herself. After we each have our tea, she moves to the pink chair across from us and shifts her body around for a few minutes without looking in our direction. My grandmother finally takes a sip from her cup, then levels her gaze on me. "What do you want to know first?"

I hesitate. I pondered questions during the entire car ride. Asking myself, if I could only have one answer, what would be the most pressing? My voice sounds shy when I finally speak, "Why haven't I met you before today?"

She audibly exhales, placing her teacup on the stack of books to her left. "It's a complicated story, Dear. Your mother is my daughter, but she renounced me years ago." My grandma pauses, reaching up her hand, allowing the cat figurine to walk off the bookshelf and onto her palm, "Her sister wished to join another Coven, in pursuit of non-traditional magics. I supported her departure and your mother never forgave either of us."

"I have an aunt?" I ask, latching onto the idea of a huge family I've never met before.

First a grandmother, then an aunt. What about an uncle or cousins? My parents always say that family is important. I love them for it, but also question the truth behind the sentiment, considering they've hidden part of our family from me.

My grandmother's face falls. "Not anymore, Dear. But you did, many years ago." She watches the small cat strut across her arm, working up to her shoulder. Once it reaches its destination, it stops moving and curls up into a small ball, closing its eyes.

When my grandmother's gaze returns to mine, pain is visible in her bright eyes. It's clear, even years later, she misses both daughters she lost. That one look makes me alter my line of questioning, deciding to ask about my deceased aunt some other time. Instead, I focus on a different portion of her response. "What did you mean by another coven that embraces other types of magic?"

My grandmother steeples her hands together in front of her. "Here in Florence, we are only able to use potions magic. According to historical texts, years ago, many types of magic were available. Including spell casting and the sight, to name a couple you've probably heard of."

I nod, eager to hear more.

"When the curse was cast on this town, it created a trickle effect that spread out to witches across the world. Magic is limited everywhere, but there are still those that seek the old ways and wish to unlock types of magic that haven't been used in centuries."

My brow furrows as I consider her words. Rather than feeling more informed, my grandmother's responses are generating even more questions. I feel so sheltered from my family and our history right now. I love my parents, but I can't believe all they've hidden from me. When my mom revealed our potion's magic, she barely even scratched the surface of information that's been withheld.

"Shouldn't every coven be trying to find a cure to this curse?" I ask, wondering why it just garners widespread acceptance.

My grandmother shrugs and the cat statue

momentarily distracts me, meowing quietly when her movement disturbs it. "Many believe we're better off this way. Your mother says that her sister and I were power hungry for trying to access more magic. To an extent, only having the ability to brew potions is safer for us, other creatures, and humans." She looks like she's struggling to find her next words. "I don't think it's wrong to attempt unlocking powers our ancestors had, that we were meant to have, if it weren't for the curse. But it's also not something that everyone believes in, and we have to accept that choice too."

"Do we keep humans from living in town?"

My grandmother chuckles. "Once a month, we spray the edges of our side with a potion. Humans can visit, but if they stay longer than a few days, they become more and more agitated and feel an urgent need to return home, or wherever they came from. It's safer for them and easier for us. We don't have to worry about trying to explain some of our oddities. The wolves don't feel the same compulsion for exclusivity, so there are some humans in Florence, but not too many."

I continue questioning my grandma, until my mind is overwhelmed, bogged down with information I'll need to wade through later. I'm glad she rescued Vlad and I and provided some additional details about our family.

As I think about Florence, and the idea that my neighbors are all witches, I realize that means Sylvia probably is too! I'm suddenly fighting the urge to dial her number, wanting to confront her about the secret.

I stifle my impulses, finishing my tea, then slowly rising from the couch. Before we exit her cottage, my grandma pulls me to the side into a warm hug and whispers in my ear, "I don't know what happened with that Eric fellow, but I have a contact I plan to reach out to. We'll find out more and fix what we can."

I nod, and she releases me with a smile.

Outside, the three of us pile into her car and Vlad states, "You can drive us to my house, it's closer."

Allowing him to take control of the situation, my thoughts wander during the short drive. My mind is full of information about witches and shifters, floating around in random nonsensical snippets that I attempt to piece together. All of this is so overwhelming and I haven't even delved into the actual potion brewing part of my ancestry.

Barely any time passes before we pull up to the Mort's. I linger for half a second, reluctant to leave the ancient Chevelle. What if I never see my grandmother again?

Like she's reading my thoughts, she offers a reassuring smile and says, "I'll be in touch soon, Dear."

Nodding, I exit the vehicle, joining Vlad on the curb. We stand together, watching and waving as she pulls away.

Once she's out of sight, Vlad steps to the side and begins a set of intense stretches on his driveway. He circles his neck and lunges deeply, apparently needing to stretch out his stiff muscles from the tiny car.

His antics cause me to giggle. It was cramped, but we were in there for six minutes, tops.

When he finally finishes loosening his muscles, he turns to me with a raised eyebrow. "Wanna come in?"

22

THE RESEARCH

Mirabella

T he following morning, I wake slightly disoriented. I'm tucked against a warm body for the second time this week, but unlike last time, the discovery is not as startling. As my mind sheds the last vestiges of sleep, I recall cuddling up with Vlad on his couch. I assume I fell asleep and he carried me into his room.

With the front of his body plastered against the back of mine, my skin is hot in all the places we touch, like Vlad is a human... err... shifter, heater. He has a leg thrown across my body and an arm tightly gripping my waist, like he was afraid I would escape in the middle of the night.

As comfortable as I am, my bladder is urgently insisting I leave the bed. I try to wriggle and worm my way away from Vlad, but am unsuccessful in escaping his tight grip. All I seem to accomplish is rubbing my butt against his crotch, causing his hand to tightly grip my hip as he emits a low groan. I pause, waiting to see if he's woken up, but his deep breathing continues.

Before I'm able to move again, Vlad uses his grip to still my hips as he slides his growing erection against my center. The movement makes my breath catch and I can't stop my back from arching into him, furthering the contact. Vlad repeats the movement, groaning again, and the noise snaps me to my senses... this is Vlad!

I push his hand away and rush to the bathroom. Gripping onto the vanity while my lungs heave, working in overdrive to keep pace with my frantic pants. I stare at my disheveled reflection in the mirror, trying to organize the chaos in my thoughts and identify the feelings budding between Vlad and I. Are we friends? Or is there something more happening here?

Unfortunately, the answer doesn't fall from the sky, appear on the mirror, or occur in any other prophetic manner. Sighing, I give up.

Pushing away from the counter, I handle my business, taking an extra long time to wash my hands while my thoughts continue to wander. I reach the point where it's weird to continue being in the bathroom any longer and finally return to the bedroom.

I stop just a few steps in, eying Vlad.

He's rolled to his back, spread across the center of the bed like a starfish, with his fingers and toes reaching out to each corner. The upper half of his body is on full display, with his blankets slung low around his hips.

My eyes wander over Vlad's sleeping form, using the opportunity to admire his broad shoulders, thickly muscled arms, and chiseled abs. Without realizing it, my feet carry me towards him, my fingers itching to slide across the small trail of hair starting on his lower belly and disappearing under the covers.

Vlad's rumbling voice interrupts my perusal. "Get back in bed, Little Mir."

Shaking my head to clear it, I lift a side of the covers, barely stopping my gaze from drifting lower. I perch gently on the edge of the bed. Not wanting to disturb Vlad as he covers the majority of the surface area, I lay down on my side, my arms tucked against me. My body is stiff, while thoughts ping rapidly through my mind.

Vlad shifts, and his arm scoops me up, depositing me atop his chest. One arm remains across my back while the other rests across my thighs. They're like bands of steel, making it clear he doesn't intend to let me leave the bed again. I'm not protesting the action. Instead, I snuggle against his chest, shutting off my brain, and allowing his heat to soothe me back to sleep.

FEELING A SENSE OF DÉJÀ VU, the smells of breakfast wafting into Vlad's room wake me sometime later. This time, Vlad remains in the bed with me, sleeping deeply, and still clasping me tightly against his body.

A knock raps on the bedroom door and Tricia's voice sings, "Are you two lovebirds awake? It's time for breakfast."

My cheeks heat with unexplained embarrassment. Vlad groans and drags his eyes open as he sits upright. Our gazes connect, and a simmering heat builds in the connection. Without looking away, Vlad rasps, "We'll be out in a minute."

His voice is still coated in sleep, but his eyes are fully open and alert. Vlad's looking at me like he can see through my clothes, straight to the skin underneath them... and he likes what he sees. The look has me swaying towards him instinctually.

Vlad closes the distance between our bodies, placing his nose against the skin of my shoulder as my body plasters against him. He runs his face up my neck, tracing a line all the way to the sensitive skin behind my ear lobe. Pausing, his tongue flits out, slicking against my skin before he places a brief hot kiss. During his retreat, he inhales deeply, then his teeth nip at my earlobe.

The brief affection has my heart pounding in my chest, and a light, throbbing pulse starts between my legs. Vlad doesn't seem to notice. He leaps out of bed and ambles to the bathroom, like he doesn't have a care in the world. Like we wake up in bed together every morning and he always kisses my neck.

Taking a deep breath to orient myself, I run a hand

through my hair and wince as it catches on a huge tangle. I take a few seconds to finger comb my long blonde locks into a more presentable arrangement for breakfast. Eventually, I give up and tie it all into a sloppy bun on the top of my head.

Looking down, I realize I must've changed before I crawled into bed. I'm wearing a giant T-shirt and a pair of Vlad's shorts. I spot my clothes heaped on top of the dresser. I waver before stepping out into the hallway, but ultimately decide not to change.

When I enter the kitchen, Tricia is manning the stove like a well-tuned machine. She's flipping pancakes and frying bacon, like she's in her natural habitat. The sight shows the similarities between her and Vlad and my last experience sleeping here.

Bart is sitting at the table, drinking a mug of coffee and holding up a copy of the *F.O. Daily*, while the sunlight glints off his shiny bald head. A plate piled high with food is already placed in front of him, and he seems preoccupied by the paper and his pancakes.

Tricia spots me lingering. She shoots a small smile as she delivers more food to the table, then immediately returns to the stove. I pause a brief second longer, then slip into the seat beside Bart and pile an empty plate with food. Ignoring the awkward feeling attempting to bubble up, I dig in, moaning as the fluffy goodness of pancakes touches my tongue.

Seconds later, Vlad joins us, now wearing a shirt. I stifle my sigh of disappointment over covering such a glorious set of abs, then watch surreptitiously as he piles his plate with enough food to feed a family of four. He clasps his fork in his left hand, but his right snakes out, grabbing onto the edge of my chair and dragging me closer. The legs loudly skid across the linoleum floor until I'm practically in Vlad's lap. He lays an arm across the back of my chair and finally eats. His knee nudges mine and I pick up my fork distractedly, wondering if Bart or Tricia will say anything.

Neither of them pays us any mind. The four of us continue on with breakfast, like Vlad and I wrapped around each other at their table is commonplace.

AFTER SOME FINAGLING, I'm driven home and Vlad picks up his car. It seems longer than twenty-four hours ago that we were dragged to Community Hall. But that's probably due to our action-packed day and the revelations from my grandmother.

Leaning against my bedroom door, I fiddle with my phone, seeking the courage I need to confront my best friend. Before I lose my nerve, I press the green call button. Sylvia picks up on the first ring, as usual.

"Girl, how was the rest of your birthday?" She screams into the phone.

Instead of answering her, I ask, "Are you a witch, Sylvia?"

Sylvia is silent. The only noise on the line is a couple of shouts from one of her brothers, but even that fades away. I glance down at my screen, checking to see if we disconnected. Sylvia's name still shows, and I place the phone back to my ear.

Eventually she releases a long, deep sigh. The sound confirms my suspicion, but she still replies, "I've known this conversation was coming for years, but it still doesn't make it any easier."

"You've known we're witches for years?!" I ask, a sense of betrayal settling deep into my bones. I keep nothing from Sylvia. She's the first person I call whenever anything happens and the only person who knows every single one of my secrets. Even the truly embarrassing ones. I can't believe she's known a life-altering secret, one that affects both of us, for years, and didn't tell me.

Sylvia's breath hits the receiver hard, the sound echoing loudly through the speaker into the silence of my bedroom. "When my parents decided to move mid-school year, I threw a huge fit. They tried all the usual tactics to help convince me: offered a new computer, the biggest room, anything. One day I overheard a strange conversation, and I was able to drag the real reason for our move out of them. We are witches and they wanted to change covens."

Her words are like pieces of hail pinging against bare skin. Although small in impact, they issue a lingering sting. The entire foundation of our friendship is based on a half-truth. Sylvia was privy to a set of secrets that involved us both, without telling me.

My thoughts are interrupted as Sylvia continues, "It wasn't until I had been here for a few months that I realized our entire side of the town is witches, including you."

Five years. For five years, Sylvia buried this information and hid it like it was a treasure. I don't respond, but she continues to spill her guts, unravelling the secrets she's kept. "I wasn't allowed to practice until my eighteenth birthday, but I've been to a few Coven events. Including solstice with my parents last month."

It takes a few seconds for the timing to click together. Then I realize her camping trip with her parents was actually a witch event. The solstice.

I feel like my life is changing momentously.

My family keeping this secret as part of their tradition didn't feel like a betrayal. Even hiding my grandmother didn't feel maliciously deceitful. To my mom, my grandma really was dead. They hadn't spoken in years, since before I was even born.

But the fact that my best friend has known for years she's a witch—that I'm one too—and kept these pieces of our lives hidden... That feels like a slice right down the center of my heart. One I'm not sure I'll recover from any time soon.

Sylvia is still rambling about her family's involvement with the coven. Her tone sounds eager while she talks about the future, how we can practice together to take our witches exams and join the coven.

I interrupt her with a firm tone, silencing her words with mine, "I'm sorry, Sylvia. I feel like I need some time."

Her words stop immediately. The next time she

speaks, her voice sounds smaller than I've ever heard from my larger-than-life friend. "What do you mean?"

This time, I release a sigh. The sound encompasses everything I wish to say, but don't quite know how. It signifies the end of something. But whether it's our friendship or a change in myself, I'm not quite sure yet. "A lot has happened recently, and I feel like I need some space to think things over."

We hang up after Sylvia agrees to give me some time, glossing over her betrayal. It suddenly feels as if the list of people I can trust is dwindling with each passing day. At this point, the only person in my life that hasn't purposefully lied to me is Vlad.

Pushing the heavy thought aside, I gather my things and head into my studio. As I'm grabbing the door handle, my phone rings. I expect it to be Sylvia again, but an unknown number prefixed with the Florence area code is flashing across the screen. Hesitating momentarily, I accept the call on what's likely the last ring on the caller's end.

Immediately after I answer, my grandmother's nasally voice flows through the phone. She sounds agitated as she speaks, "Hello, Dear. Something's come up. I need to see you as soon as possible. Will you and Vlad come by this afternoon?"

"Is everything okay?" I ask, concerned.

"Yes, yes, Dear. Even the trees have ears. Just come by and we can talk about it here."

Brushing off her odd phrase, I agree, "Okay, we'll be there in a few hours. Can I have your address?"

She chuckles into my ear and responds, "I live in a tree, Dear, I don't have an address. Have Vlad drive you. Tell him to take the road to the old trailhead and turn at the large boulder three miles in, he'll be able to find his way here."

She sounds confident in Vlad's navigation abilities, so I agree. "Okay, we'll see you soon."

We exchange a few more words, then she hangs up. I shoot Vlad a text and ask if he'll be available in a couple hours. Immediately, I see the three dots appear, indicating he's typing back. I receive a quick but brief "yes" in response.

VLAD DRIVES my Prius to my grandmother's treehouse, as it's a tiny bit better-suited for the bumpy dirt road than his low sports car. He follows her instructions, and it doesn't take long before the enormous tree comes into sight.

We pull into the small dirt patch, parking next to her ancient Chevelle. My grandma is waiting on the porch for us, silently opening the door as we approach. After ushering us in, she tells us to seat ourselves, rushing off to the kitchen to make tea.

Glancing around, I see that not much has changed since yesterday. The pens and scrolls have been cleared from the coffee table, and a much larger pile of books has taken their place. Other than that, the living space looks the same as before.

Today the wait seems shorter. My grandmother

bustles back in with her tea tray, handing each of us a cup before settling into her pink armchair.

"Dear, I'm concerned about the wolves," she starts, holding my gaze steadily for a moment before moving onto Vlad. "They're more desperate than I originally thought yesterday." She pauses dramatically, taking a long sip of tea. She releases a satisfied sigh as she moves her cup away from her lips.

I tap my foot against the floor, a nervous habit I sometimes give in to. I'm impatient for her to continue and tell us the reason behind her call. My grandmother looks pointedly at my leg, with her teacup half raised to her lips. Vlad places a warm palm on my thigh to soothe the tension that's building and I stop jiggling.

My grandma releases another small sigh. "It seems a wave of shifters have recently gotten stuck as wolves. Even ones that didn't appear to be resisting the change. The Council thinks you're the answer to their problems. If this continues, I won't be able to stop them from coming after you again."

"But-t, I already tried. I'm, I'm not able to help," I stammer out, her words stirring a heady combination of surprise and trepidation. Everyone saw what happened yesterday. It's clear I'm not the cure they're searching for. Why would the wolf Council still want me?

"I believe you Dear, but unfortunately it doesn't seem like the Council does." She pauses again, sipping on her tea, setting her cup down, then settling deeper into the armchair, all before she resumes speaking. "My contact finally got in touch. I'll be heading out of town for a week or so to find some answers. Hopefully, I'll gather information on the curse, the shifters, and the claims of the young man, Eric."

I watch as my grandma's shrewd eyes search Vlad's face. He holds her gaze and a minute later she nods, as if she's glimpsed into his soul and found an answer that satisfied her.

She turns to look at me again, then points to the stack of books on the table. "These are some texts that may help our search. I'd like you two to come by here each day, after work or any other obligations you currently have. I need you to look through these and search for clues on how this shifter issue involves the Coven and, more importantly, you."

My grandma slowly rises from the pink chair and refills her cup. She throws a pointed look at the two still-full teacups. Her message is clear. I gently lift mine, taking a small sip. It tastes like cinnamon and instantly warms me from the inside out.

She smiles at me, pleased, then continues talking, "It's important that you keep up appearances, it needs to look as if nothing's changed. Don't skip work to come here or tell anyone else what we've talked about today. Not even your parents."

Pausing again, she sips on her tea. Her communication is infuriatingly dramatic, she draws out the conversation, knowing she holds our attention completely.

"Bookmark any important information you find for my review once I've returned. And lastly, don't remove the books from the house. They're invaluable and we can't have them falling into the wrong hands during such dire times."

I nod once, seeing Vlad do the same out of the corner of my eye.

Her cryptic words and demands have me more fearful than my trip to Community Hall or the giant, feral wolf put before me by the Shifter Council. I have a feeling that things are going to continue moving rapidly downhill from here, while gaining speed. And there will be nothing to stop the mess from splattering against the quickly approaching rock bottom.

I hope my grandmother returns with answers before the Council seeks me out again.

23

THE EXPO

Mirabella

Obviously, the Council is hiding the wolf issue for their own reasons. Maybe to avoid widespread panic or possibly for some other, unknown, purpose. Either way, Vlad and I don't want to be the ones to metaphorically let the wolf out of the bag by suddenly quitting our jobs and spending all our time in the woods together.

Following my grandma's advice, we both show up to work the next day, as usual. The second I step through the doors, Glenna rushes up to me. "I thought you'd never get here, honey. Today's the day! We need to get moving. The knitting expo waits for no one!" She's beaming from ear to ear, practically dancing with joy. If it wasn't already clear from her prior weeks of stories about the event, the knitting expo is clearly the highlight of her year.

Meanwhile, I'm stifling a groan, not wanting to rain on her parade. I'm not mentally prepared to deal with the kooks at the expo today. I try to force a smile on my face for Glenna's sake, but I'm obviously not successful.

Her brow furrows, and she asks in a concerned tone, "Are you okay, honey?" In a quieter voice, she continues, "Your face reminds me of the time that I ate bad shrimp. Did you eat any shrimp recently?"

I work on shifting my expression to appear happier, but eventually give up with a sigh. My lips are stuck in a down turned grimace at this point. "I'm fine. I just didn't sleep well, but I'm sure I'll feel better at the expo. Is there no morning meeting today?" I ask, hoping there is one to delay the inevitable just a bit longer.

Glenna drops her concerned expression, thoughts of my potential illness rapidly fleeing. She claps her hands together before excitedly striding to the door with jaunty steps. "We get to skip it for the expo! Let's get a move on, we need to hurry to catch anything newsworthy."

Her steps rapidly carry her to the door. It's the fastest I've seen her move in the weeks I've worked here. When she reaches the exit, she looks over her shoulder, "Are you coming, honey?"

Quietly exhaling a deep breath, I focus on clearing my expression. I walk to the door with determined steps, like this isn't a death sentence.

Maybe the expo won't be that bad.

. . .

IT'S WORSE than I expected.

The warehouse hosting the expo is absolute chaos. A collection of assorted people, miscellaneous goods, loud noises, and pungent smells. Old people with walkers clog up the aisles, running over any stray toes that dare to get in their way. Fighting through the congestion, I follow Glenna the best I can, but she seems to have better luck dodging the masses.

Vendors are yelling over each other about their wares, some stepping into the aisle ways and adding to the traffic, just to be seen and heard. I might be deaf in my left ear, after I accidentally walked past a man with a megaphone yelling, "Extra thick yarn, made of alpaca, available over here!" And that was four steps into the building.

Once we're past the first few booths of goods, we walk between vendors selling food. For some reason, a fried pickles booth was placed right next to a stand serving cotton candy. The two smells in close proximity create a stench that makes me gag as I pass by. Like a sweet and salty vinegar dough ball crawled into my nostrils. The smell follows me, lingering and unescapable.

After a single aisle, I'm ready to hightail it back to the parking lot, but there's five more rows just like the first one. I long for my safe and odor free desk back at the Daily. The thought, *I'm an intern. I'm not even being paid to be here!* Is playing on loop in my brain.

Once we left the Daily, Glenna shoved her pen and a pad of paper into her purse, dropping the pretense she was eager about the journalistic opportunity. She's in hog heaven, grinning from ear to ear, her head swiveling to look at everything all at once, as she strides with spry steps.

She flits in and out of the tents, examining goods as I struggle through mobs of people that don't want to let me pass. She's already made me feel yarn with her three separate times, asking me to offer my opinions on her purchases, when I'm able to catch up with her quick pace.

Meanwhile, I'm trying to think of a feasible excuse to get me out of this place.

By the time we've wound our way through the first two rows of booths, each hosting about twenty vendors, my feet are pulsing. The hard, concrete floor is brutalizing my feet through my sandals and I wish I'd known about this plan in advance, to choose better footwear, or maybe call in sick.

Not to be a whiny brat, but I am absolutely miserable. Plenty of people enjoy the events in Florence, like the expo, but personally I'd rather be... anywhere else. The second the thought crosses my mind, an elbow hits me in the face. Ducking, I barely dodge a knitting needle sailing through the air in an arc, scarcely missing my eye.

Startled, I glance in the assaulter's direction. My eyes land on the back of a graying head of hair. The man responsible doesn't turn to look at me, instead he picks up another knitting needle, swinging it in the air erratically.

I back away, cautiously, concerned I may be on the end of a knitting expo stabbing if I move too quickly. I briefly consider texting Sylvia SOS, but I'm not sure I'm ready to forgive her, yet.

Snagging my phone from my pocket, I type: **SOS.**

Three dots immediately show on my screen, Vlad's message appearing shortly after: **Is it the Council? Are you in trouble?**

Raising my eyes from my phone, I connect with Glenna's gaze. She motions for me to meet her at a bamboo knitting needle booth. Wary of elderly folk swinging sharp objects, I swipe a response with my left thumb while keeping my eyes on the pathway. **Worse. Knitting expo. Send help, ASAP.**

He responds with several laughing emojis, and I groan. Vlad won't be any help. He confirms my assumption with a second message: **Could be worse. Bring back some good snacks.**

"Honey, are you having fun? Look at these bamboo needles, they're fantastic," Glenna says the second I step into the booth.

Running my fingers across one briefly, I nod. "They're very nice. I think I spotted a lemonade stand while I was walking here. I'm going to grab a drink. Do you want anything?"

She waves a hand over her shoulder in response, already shoving through a swarm of geriatrics to enter the next booth she's set her sights on.

Shaking my head, I stride in the direction of the stand topped by a giant lemon. The queue is pretty long, but the amount of people waiting doesn't deter me. It probably means that the drink is delicious. Plus, the wait will relieve me from analyzing the merits of alpaca versus sheep yarn with Glenna.

Every time I catch up to her, she offers me options, comparing and contrasting swatches of yarn or knitting needles and asking for my input. Every single thing here looks the same, like either yarn or knitting needles. It will be nice to have a break.

While in line, I scroll through my social media. Tuning out the chaos surrounding me, to look at pictures of people I barely know. It helps to pass the time, and within ten minutes, I'm holding a strawberry lemonade.

Tucking myself against the side of the stand to avoid being jostled, I take my first sip. The sweet, tangy liquid hits my tongue and I moan. This lemonade almost makes the trauma of the expo worth it. Almost.

I take a few more sips, then move into the center of the aisle to look for Glenna. Thankfully, people diverge around me, like I'm a median in the human traffic and I'm able to spot her gray bun popping in and out of the booths near the emergency exit. I finish my lemonade, tossing the paper cup into the bin, then move in her direction.

Fewer people pepper the furthest aisle. Therefore, the insanity of the expo is less apparent and my search for Glenna involves less toe-stepping chaos. I almost find myself having fun as I peek my head into each of the fabric tents, scanning the goods as I hunt her down.

I'm approaching the last tent when screams erupt. My relaxed feeling immediately flees and I pivot in the direction of the noise. Before my body completes the turn, my eyes connect with the dark gaze of a massive, brown-furred wolf bounding around the corner and into my aisle.

Rooted in place, I watch as people dive out of the way to avoid the rampaging beast. Time moves in slow motion as he pauses, eyes locked on mine. The wolf snarls, baring his teeth as spittle pools on the ground beneath him. He bends his front legs, like he's preparing to leap a hundred yards in my direction.

Slowly, without turning, I back towards the exit door. My movement doesn't escape his notice. The wolf releases a low, deep warning growl. Even with the distance between us, I feel the noise rumbling down my spine, activating my fight or flight instincts.

I choose flight.

Twirling around, I scramble towards the exit, with sloppy, fear-filled movements, as the wolf barrels towards me. My terror causes me to stumble, and I hit the floor with a terrified shriek. The noise of the wolf's paws pounding against the hard cement of the expo floor become audible as he nears.

My fear amps up as I realize I won't reach the door in time to escape. Panic floods my brain and in a split-second decision, I curl around myself in a ball, trying to make as small a target as possible, preparing for the worst.

The growling, which has been a constant noise for the past... however long, unexpectedly ceases. I curl tighter around myself, expecting to be bit any second. But the silence lingers, the lack of noise deafening.

After a few more minutes, I uncover my head and risk a peek over my shoulder. My eyes widen in shock at the sight that greets me.

The golden wolf from the Community Hall is now standing between me and the wolf with the brown fur. He looks like he's... guarding me. Protecting me against the rabid creature that somehow found his way inside the expo.

My golden wolf is still wearing the metal muzzle from the other day. Dangling from the chains are two metal circles, with large pieces of plaster attached. It looks like the wolf broke off a portion of the wall attached to his chains in order to escape.

The brown wolf interrupts my thoughts, snagging my attention as he lunges forward, snarling. My concern shifts to the golden wolf, his mouth still covered by his muzzle, unable to snap back at his opponent.

The golden wolf rears onto his hind legs, lashing out with his front paws. He creates deep slices across the side of the brown wolf as he lunges again. Blood drips down the wolf's side, pooling on the floor, but the brown wolf is undeterred.

My golden wolf howls as the brown wolf prepares

to attack again. The sound is haunting, echoing through the expo and raising the small hairs on my arms and spine. The noise is powerful and dominant. It cows the brown wolf, causing him to kneel and whimper, then hightail it out of sight.

My wolf stands in front of me, like a sentinel. He watches until the brown wolf disappears from view. The second he's gone; my wolf turns to face me. I slowly rise from the floor, wary any quick movements might cause the wolf to lash out.

A set of vibrant green eyes watch as I stand. I slowly extend my right palm, allowing him time to move out of the way if he doesn't want to be touched. The wolf remains in place, watching me. With a deep inhale, my palm connects with the fur on his neck. My golden wolf chuffs, stepping forward and nuzzling my side with his snout.

"Thank you," I whisper, outwardly calm as I swipe my hand through his fur, my fingers tangling in the long, matted strands.

The motion slightly soothes the thoughts pinging through my brain. Foremost being, who is this wolf and why is he here? I barely contain the words, even knowing the wolf can't answer.

With one more chuff and nuzzle, my golden wolf bounds away. My eyes track his movements as he exits the expo, following the same path as the brown wolf.

As he disappears from sight, I become aware of the lingering silence in the expo building. All around me, people are slowly and silently beginning to rise from the ground and emerge from booths that escaped the wrath of the wolves. I watch as people attempt to re-erect tents and reconnect with loved ones.

As time passes, a low, steady murmur of voices gradually becomes audible. My gaze drifts around, absorbing the shocked and confused faces of people milling about, as we all try to make sense of the incident.

24

THE DAILY

Mirabella

Glenna drives us back to the Daily. Expo officials shut down the event to provide vendors time to recoup from the damage. It's estimated booths won't be ready to reopen for at least a week, but they postponed the expo until further notice.

The events of this afternoon were so bizarre. Glenna can't stop raving about it. "This is the greatest story ever. And I was involved. I can't wait to get back and start writing," she exclaims, for the fifteenth time.

I'm too shaken to respond, so I nod instead. For the fifteenth time.

The adrenaline has seeped out of my body, leaving me exhausted with even more questions than before.

Suddenly, Glenna stops talking. The lack of her constant chatter makes the silence startling and I glance up from the dashboard to assess the situation. We're at a stoplight, but nothing appears remiss. Concerned, I glance to my left and find Glenna staring at me with an unreadable expression.

She finally asks, "Don't you think that was strange?" I begin to nod, but she continues, "The brown wolf became so focused on you almost immediately. He left everyone else alone and appeared to target you. Why?"

I do think it's strange, and I'm not sure why.

To Glenna I respond, "I was directly in his path and panicked. I think I activated his predatory instincts when I bolted for the exit door." My voice sounds shaky and breathless, revealing just how upset I still am.

Glenna considers my words, then nods vigorously. "That makes sense and was very unlucky. At least that other one stepped in. Did you see the chains, though? I wonder if the pair escaped from the zoo, or maybe they were pets..."

Ignoring Glenna, I wiggle my phone out of my pocket and type out a quick message to Vlad while concealing the screen under my right thigh. Things keep escalating and we need answers. **Returning from Expo. Meet in parking lot, 10 min.**

He responds with a thumbs up and I exhale the breath I didn't realize I was holding.

It only takes eight minutes for Glenna to pull into the lot for the Daily, but Vlad is already waiting. The second she places the car in park, I leap from her vehicle. Glenna is slower to get out, moving at her normal pace, versus the expedited one she used this morning.

Gesturing to Vlad, I say, "I'm going to go talk, I'll be inside in a few."

She nods, continuing towards the Daily at the pace of a slug. I wait until she's stepped into the building; the door closing gently behind her, then I rush Vlad. He meets me halfway, catching me as I throw myself at him, wrapping my arms around his neck and melding our bodies together.

He lifts me up, squeezing my body tightly against his as one of his hands sweeps down my back in a soothing motion. I feel him nuzzle into my hair, inhaling deeply, before he returns my feet to the ground.

I bask in his warmth for a second longer, before I blurt out, "A wolf rampaged through the expo, then-thegoldenwolffromthecouncilcametorescueme," The words all tumble together, in my haste to get them out, but it doesn't seem to matter.

Vlad separates from me slightly, just enough for his amber gaze to search mine. "Are you okay?" His eyes run down my body, or the parts visible due to our proximity. "Did they hurt you at all?"

I shake my head firmly. "The golden wolf... was still wearing the muzzle." I pause. "It was like he ripped out part of the wall to chase after the brown wolf. All to save me at the expo."

Vlad rubs his palms up and down my arms in a soothing motion, his brow furrowed while he contemplates my words. He finally responds, slowly, as if the thought is forming while he speaks, "There's still so much for us to learn. We'll go to your grandmother's tonight and look through the books she left for us. We'll find answers, Little Mir."

I open my mouth to respond, but I'm interrupted by a throat clearing loudly behind me. Vlad's head shoots up and a scowl instantly mars his face. I turn slowly, detaching his arms, suspecting the identity of the person to invoke such a negative reaction, so quickly, from Vlad.

Marc is waiting with his arms across his chest. He doesn't immediately meet my gaze. He appears bashful, like he interrupted a make-out session instead of an admittedly intimate conversation.

Crap. Why did I have to think about kissing Vlad?

Suddenly, I feel like I have to avoid Marc's gaze as the vivid image of Vlad's plump lips connecting with mine floods my brain.

Marc clears his throat again, and I shake my head, hoping to bring my thoughts back to the present. "Mira, I uh heard about what happened at the expo, just now, from Glenna. I wanted to come and check if you were alright," he states, taking a half step in my direction.

He uncrosses his arms, and his hands pulse by his side. He fists them, like he's fighting the urge to gather me into his arms. I glance at Vlad, feeling torn.

Do I go to Marc and thank him for checking on me? It's really a sweet gesture for him to come out here, but I don't want to give the wrong impression. Marc is probably the most thoughtful guy I've met, but we lack the magnetic attraction that exists between Vlad and I.

With Marc, it's different.

I feel so comfortable around him and I'm reluctant to let him go. I frown as I realize eventually it will come to that. I will have to choose between Vlad and Marc, maybe even right this second, in this parking lot. I will have to make a choice.

Opening my mouth to respond, I'm cut off by an abrasive sounding Vlad. "Yeah man, she's fine. I'm about to drive her home."

Marc narrows his eyes before cutting his gaze to me. "Would you rather I drive you home? I'll pick you up in the morning and bring you to work tomorrow. You're on my way here."

Indignation blooms across Vlad's face, and his shoulders shake lightly with rage. Placing my hand against his chest to ground him and keep his wolf at bay, I respond to Marc. "I'm fine riding with Vlad. My mom can bring me in the morning. My parents have been asking about the Morts for a few days now, anyway."

I smile, knowing the expression doesn't reach my eyes, but hoping to soften the blow of my words. I hate lying to Marc, not only because he's my boss, but also my... friend. "You should probably help Glenna, anyway. The expo needs to be front page tomorrow!"

Marc's eyes dance between my slightly strained, lying smile and Vlad's furious face. He turns back to the Daily with a small audible huff, but doesn't protest any further.

A pang of sadness hits my chest as Marc strides inside. His shoulders are tense, his fists clenched by his side. His posture makes it clear things between us just became infinitely more complicated. I don't want any strain between Marc and I. I really like him... just possibly in a different way than I like Vlad.

Vlad tugs on my arm, and I pivot to face him. Tabling my thoughts of Marc for later, I whisper, "Let's go to the treehouse."

WE SPEND hours poring over the tomes left by my grandmother. I skim through pages of information, my finger trailing over the text seeking any mentions of shifters, witches, magic or curses.

My eyes begin to blur, weary from constant use. Slamming the cover of my book, I fight off a feeling of hopelessness. I'm exhausted, starving, and feel like this afternoon was a waste of time. We found nothing relevant, at all.

Vlad's warm palm finds mine, startling me from my thoughts of despair. "It'll be okay, Little Mir. We will find answers. But for tonight, let's call it quits and grab something to eat."

I squeeze his hand tightly, thankful for his reassurance. He helps me to my feet and I wrap my arms low around his waist, squeezing him tightly against me.

Vlad places his chin atop my head, his voice

rumbling through my skull when he speaks. "Wanna go to the Diner? We can grab some late night burgers and shakes." It's on the tip of my tongue to decline, but Vlad continues, "It's late enough it should be empty. Everyone our age will be partying by this point."

Reluctantly, I nod against his chest. Hopefully, he's right.

Vlad takes a step back, his arms low around my waist and his amber eyes meeting my gray gaze. "What do you say we get some greasy food tonight, then tomorrow you let me take you out?"

"What would we be doing tonight?" I ask, distractedly, as his face inches closer to mine, like it's uncontrollable. The heat from his gaze is so intense, I'm surprised the look isn't singing my eyelashes.

"Tonight, is just food. Tomorrow is a proper date, Little Mir."

25

THE DATE

Mirabella

I wake slowly, a huge grin already splitting my face. Tonight, Vlad is taking me on a date. My first real date. Swinging my legs over the edge of my bed, I stand and do a little jig, swinging my hips back and forth while my hair flies around me in a halo.

My first date!

The words replay on repeat until my excitement devolves into panic. What am I going to wear?

I pick up my phone, my fingers immediately hovering over Sylvia's name. I pause, torn. This is a situation where I need my best friend's help, but am I ready to forgive her for betraying my trust? She's already proven that she has no qualms about keeping secrets from me. What if she does it again? What if she hurts me again?

Inhaling deeply, I choose forgiveness.

Life is about taking chances on people and hoping they don't disappoint. Sylvia messed up, but she isn't a terrible person. Maybe just a good one that made a bad decision.

Without giving myself a chance to change my mind, I text a single word: **SOS.**

Immediately after clicking send, my phone trills. Sylvia's name flashing across the screen in time with the noise. With a calming breath, I accept the call. "Hey Sylv."

"Mir, let's never fight again," she begs.

"Deal," I reply, without hesitation.

This is my best friend, my number one supporter, my ride or die. Hearing her voice makes me realize how much I've missed her, even though it hasn't been that long since our last conversation.

"Now, I need your help." I pause. "I have a date."

She squeals loudly into my ear and I swear I can hear her jumping up and down, the phone rustling against her hair with the motion. "When, where, with who?" She shouts in quick succession.

I laugh affectionately, enjoying her enthusiasm. I've really missed her. Not just recently, but this entire summer. It's the first time we've spent so many days apart since I met her.

"It's tonight after work, at the Italian restaurant, with Vlad. But I don't know what to wear... help!" I reply in a pitiful tone.

Sylvia hmms in response. I wait her out, knowing

something good is coming next. "I'll come over at four! I have the perfect dress in my closet."

THE WORKDAY PASSES in slow motion. My gaze is frequently drawn to the clock, willing time to move faster so I can leave. Out of the corner of my eye, I see Vlad checking the same clock at least as many times as I do.

When work finally ends, we both jump up from our desks and rush out to the parking lot. I attempt to pass Vlad, but he pushes his long legs harder and quickly outpaces me. We're both laughing and out of breath by the time we reach our cars. I wave to him before hopping into my Prius and zooming off to my house, to see Sylvia and her date night outfit.

She's waiting inside my room when I arrive, lounging on my bed and yelling random things at her phone as she scrolls. A feeling of nostalgia wells inside me. I couldn't wait for high school to be over, but now I almost miss it. At the very least, I miss spending my time with my bestie.

I walk over to her and wrap an arm around her body, squeezing as tightly as I can.

Sylvia places her phone on the bed, smiling up at me. Her gaze slides past my face to my closet door. I follow her line of sight and spot a black garment bag.

"Is this it?"

She nods and I tentatively approach the bag, like walking too quickly will cause it to disappear. Holding my breath, I slide open the zipper and reveal a long, flowy black dress with thin straps and a gauzy overlay. It looks beautiful and sophisticated.

"I love it!" I gasp out.

Sylvia helps me with the dress and curls my long blonde hair before twisting it into an elegant updo. After applying minimal makeup, I have just a few minutes to spare before Vlad will be here to pick me up.

"I'm so nervous," I whisper, as I admire myself in the vanity mirror.

"Why?" Sylvia asks.

I allow my thoughts to briefly wander, then shrug. I'm not sure how to respond. How do I explain my feelings for Vlad in a few words?

Sylvia nods. Understanding on some level, she grabs my hands and jumps gently. "Come on, jump with me. It will help get rid of your nerves."

Laughing, I bounce on my toes with her, careful not to ruin my hair. After a few seconds, I surprisingly feel better.

"Good thing your parents are out or this would be worse," Sylvia states.

"Agreed." Thankfully, my mom and dad are out with Tricia and Bart at some Bingo Night. Their absence was unplanned, but now I don't have to deal with the added pressure of either set of parents hovering.

The doorbell rings, interrupting our conversation, and another wave of nerves threatens to take over.

Sylvia squeezes my hands, helping to keep them at bay. "You've got this girl."

I nod, returning the squeeze with a grin. Gathering my wits, I saunter down the stairs into the foyer, hoping to make an entrance. Stopping at the third from last step, I strike a pose with my hand on my hip.

Vlad's reaction doesn't disappoint. His eyes widen as he watches me descend the last few stairs. He fidgets with his collar, appearing equally nervous. My eyes leave his, soaking in his black, form-fitted suit. He isn't wearing a tie, and has the top few buttons undone. He looks like a total playboy.

When I reach the bottom step, he offers me a bunch of pale pink peonies. I take them, smiling at him stupidly. "Hi."

He grins back softly. "Hey."

I'm not sure how long we stand there. Gray eyes connected with amber. I get lost in the emotions swirling around in the bronze-colored orbs. There's heat, but something else. Something that I'm not ready to name, not yet.

Jacob appears in my peripherals. The flash of his gray hair, startles me out of the intense stare down with Vlad. I redirect my attention as Jacob states, "I will take those, Miss Love."

"Oh, thank you Jacob," I reply, handing him the flowers, my cheeks flushing lightly over being caught staring at Vlad like a ninny.

Jacob nods and rounds the corner out of sight. My

eyes return to Vlad and he offers me a bent elbow. "Are you ready, Little Mir?"

I nod and place my arm in his, allowing him to escort me to his car and help me inside. The second he starts the car, soft jazz music drifts from the speakers. The grin he aims in my direction makes it clear he preplanned the song.

By the time Vlad parks at the restaurant, my nervousness from earlier has faded. Tonight feels like every other time we've hung out, just in nicer clothes.

"Stay put," Vlad instructs.

Following directions, I wait, watching as Vlad rounds the car and opens my door. He takes my hand, passing the tiniest amount of static electricity as he helps me stand. I look up into his amber gaze and move a half step closer. Vlad tilts his face forward, his breath fanning over my face as our eyes remain locked.

His face inches nearer, and my eyelids droop, preparing instinctually for a kiss. Our first kiss.

Vlad chuckles, and I feel the warm sound almost as much as I hear it. "Not yet, Little Mir," he whispers. "It's time to eat."

My eyes fly open and catch his gaze. A twinkling amusement glints back at me, then he retreats. Using our connected hands, he leads me into the restaurant. The hostess eyes Vlad, completely ignoring my presence, as she escorts us to a bistro table covered in a lush white tablecloth.

A possessiveness rages through me when she winks at Vlad while placing our leather-bound menus on the table. Before I snarl at her, Vlad reaches across the table, capturing my hand in his. The action soothes my desire to stake a claim.

As the hostess walks away, Vlad chuckles, but I ignore him. Flipping open my menu, I scan the names of fancy Italian dishes instead.

AFTER OUR MEAL, we take advantage of the balmy weather and walk downtown. When we reach the center fountain, Vlad stops near a bench and tugs me into his lap as he sits. He rests a palm against my cheek, his thumb caressing my chin.

"I've wanted a night like this for a long time, Little Mir. Thank you," he whispers.

He leans closer, and I hold my breath, wondering if he's teasing me again.

He isn't.

Vlad's plump lips brush lightly against mine. The touch is tentative, like he's wordlessly ensuring the action is acceptable.

I arch into him, seeking more, and Vlad delivers. His lips seal to mine in a claiming kiss. Licking and nipping at the seams of my mouth until my lips part.

His low groan is swallowed by our kiss as his tongue sweeps across mine. Vlad digs his hands into my hair and I moan as his drugging kisses continue. I wriggle and arch, attempting to meld my body to his.

Vlad lifts me, changing our positions so I'm straddling his lap. His hands spread across my lower back, the tips of his fingers grazing my butt as he devours me. The warmth of his skin seeps through the thin fabric of my dress and heat blooms low in my belly.

I moan again, sounding embarrassingly out of breath. Vlad pulls back, pecking my lips gently, then resting his forehead against mine. I open my eyes, drinking in his handsome face as we both pant.

Vlad uses his grip to gently place me on my feet, then stands himself. I surreptitiously watch as he adjusts himself, feeling smug satisfaction that I wasn't the only one affected by our kiss.

He grabs my hand again and leads us to his car, stopping briefly by the door for another chaste peck.

The drive to my house passes quickly. I fight off a pang of disappointment when Vlad pulls up my steep driveway and parks behind my Prius. He walks me to my door and I look up, expectantly.

Vlad is staring at me intensely, like I'm a puzzle he can't solve.

Taking control, I wrap my arms around his neck and force his face to meet mine. Our lips connect in a searing kiss that I never want to end. Vlad eventually pulls away with a groan.

"You're trouble, Little Mir," he mutters against my lips.

26

THE CURE

Mirabella

Vlad and I spend every waking moment of our spare time devouring the information in the massive books left at my grandmother's cottage. With each passing day, we grow more antsy, as nothing of use is found. I'm anxious for my grandma to return with answers. The fate of the town is resting on her contact.

At almost midnight on Friday, Vlad and I are still at the tree house finishing up another long night of research. I close the book on my lap with a sigh, eyeing the remaining few left untouched, piled in front of us.

Vlad shuts the text on his lap, placing it atop the growing stack of useless books. He captures my hand in his, tugging me towards him. With a squeal, I fall into his lap and wrap my arms around his neck.

His gaze is intense before he leans forward, placing his nose in the crook of my neck and inhaling deeply. He whispers under my ear, "I think we need a break from this place. Come to brunch with me at the Diner tomorrow."

I shudder, recalling my experience with the flying food, but nod my head anyway. "It will be nice to take a break." I glance around my grandmother's eclectic home, my eyes skimming over the enormous stacks of books.

"I feel like we aren't making any progress, to be completely honest," I say, on a sigh. We've been looking for anything that could help for a week, but almost every book omits any details of the curse. "At this point, I'm hoping my grandmother's lead works out, because it's feeling like she may be the last hope we have for a cure."

Vlad nods, then rests his forehead against mine. "It will be okay, Little Mir. I have faith, and you should too."

I nod, trying to believe in his words and my grand-mother's contact.

Together we clean up our mess and leave the cluttered room. As I'm locking the door, a pair of headlights appear on the winding dirt path that leads to my grandmother's treehouse. I put my hand above my eyes, like I'm blocking the sun, hoping to identify the make of the car.

The vehicle finally reaches the end of the road and

the lights blink out. My grandmother pops out of her old Chevelle that's seen better days. "Oh good! You're both still here," she says, her nasally voice carrying on the wind. "Come help this old lady bring these things in."

She pops the trunk as we head down the steps. I peer inside and see a large pewter cauldron and a few cardboard banker boxes with closed lids. "Is this the cure?" I ask excitedly.

Grandmother shoots me a look before glancing around the woods. "Even the trees have ears, my dear. Let's get these things inside, then we'll talk about my trip."

We each grab something from the trunk and carry it up the stairs. We're forced to wait at the top while I try to balance my box and unlock the door simultaneously. It takes four trips to bring everything in from my grandmother's car. By the time we're finished, I feel as if my arms are about to fall off.

My grandmother continues to putter around after the last trip, making tea. I haven't known her for long, but I can tell she enjoys building suspense. Any attempts to rush her won't do anything to move her along.

She finally loads up a tray, placing it on the coffee table before sitting down in the pink armchair. Vlad and I are already settled into our usual couch, watching her intently while we wait.

She inhales a deep breath, then launches into her

story. "I met with the Coven in Canada, where my contact lives. Their powers differ from some other witches. They're very strong and believe if they meet you, they could identify a way to break the curse."

I jump off the couch, brimming with excitement. "What are we waiting for, Grandma? Let's go right now." I pull out my phone. "I'll call my parents and text Marc in the morning... I can just say I had an emergency and won't be at the Daily next week. I'm just an intern anyway..." I'm rambling on as thoughts flutter through my mind.

My grandmother did it.

The words bring clarity and I stop pacing, allowing relief to overcome my joy. Together we'll save Garth and any other wolves affected. We'll keep it from spreading further.

This is it.

My grandmother holds a hand in the air, halting my thoughts in their tracks. Her face is unexpectedly somber, considering her news. "Hold on, Dear." She states, looking pointedly at the couch.

I plop back down next to Vlad, accidentally whacking him with my arm during my rapid descent. He releases a sharp exhale, but my grandmother and I both ignore him.

"Why aren't we leaving immediately?" I ask.

"It's not that simple," my grandmother begins. "There are witch laws in place."

I open my mouth to reply, but quickly snap my jaw shut after she shoots a glare my way. Apparently, that was another one of her dramatic pauses, which she does not take kindly to being interrupted.

After an appropriately long pause, my grandmother continues. "Before you can travel to another Coven, you have to join your own. To do that, you must take the test for your witching license. Leaving to visit another Coven without doing this reflects poorly upon you. Like you're searching for a new place to live or for a new coven. You won't be welcomed back, if you do that."

"There are no exceptions? What if we explain the situation?"

"No exceptions," my grandmother says firmly, "But I've brought you everything that you need for the next few weeks. I'll help you practice, learn, and pass your witches exams." She gestures at the large cauldron and the boxes we carried up from her car.

I nod my head, eyeing her cottage and imagining brewing potions here. It will be a tight squeeze to unload all of those boxes, yet alone brew a potion without catching the entire tree on fire, but I'm willing to try if it means saving my town.

"Okay, what do we do first?"

Grandmother chuckles as she stands from her chair. "It's late now. You two go home and get some rest." She walks to the door, holding it open as a not-so-subtle reinforcement of her words. "We'll talk again tomorrow, Dear. We need to bring all our supplies to your parent's Witching Chamber. It's safest to practice there."

Vlad and I step out onto the front porch, per her request, and the door shuts firmly behind us. As we walk towards my car, I see a flash of movement amongst the trees.

"Did you see that?" I whisper, pointing in the movement's direction.

"No," Vlad whispers back, just as quietly.

I can tell he's now on high alert. His shoulders are tense, with his ears listening intently for any threats. We both hear the twig snapping at the same time, our heads twisting toward whatever's coming.

The golden wolf, now free from the muzzle, and two others step forward, emerging from the tree line simultaneously. The three wolves sit in a line about twenty yards away. Lifting their snouts to the air, they release a long howl before flipping over to show us their bellies.

I'm bewildered, unsure of what kind of wolf protocol this is.

When I look at Vlad, his expression matches my own. "Are they submitting... to our dominance? To your dominance?" I ask, wondering if this is some weird wolf-ish show of trust.

Another howl echoes out into the night air as my only response, then suddenly Vlad leaps towards the wolves below us. His movement is too quick for me to catch, but four paws covered in dark, downy fur land on the ground seconds later.

The black-furred beast turns to look at me, a set of amber eyes connecting with mine briefly. Then, the four wolves take off, their paws ripping up the dirt as they sprint into the forest.

To Be Continued...

(Keep reading for a sneak peek at Bound: The Curse Trilogy Book 2, available now on Amazon!)

Mirabella

One pinch of blan-something leaves," I mutter to myself, reading the instructions from a potion's manual. Pulling the jar of blan... something leaves closer, I read the name off the front to confirm the ingredient. Blancara leaves. I repeat the words a few times, trying to pronounce it correctly, then grab what I estimate to be a pinch. Dropping the leaves into my cauldron with one hand, I cross the fingers on my other, hoping the spell works.

A small popping noise echoes across the chamber.

Then, nothing.

I stir a few more times, eyes widening as the golden colored liquid transitions to a murky green. This is it! I'm mastering my first potion! I clap my hands together giddily, then pull my potions manual towards me to quadruple check I haven't missed any steps.

I'm mentally checking off each direction while I read, muttering the words as my finger traces them down the page. My distraction keeps me from noticing the green smoke billowing out of the cauldron.

A slight tickle hits my throat and I cough lightly. The movement provides only a brief reprieve from the itchy feeling crawling through my esophagus.

Next thing I know, it feels like I've swallowed a furball. I clear my throat twice, but the feeling only intensifies.

Suddenly, I can't breathe. I'm gasping for air through the thick feeling clogging my throat. I begin choking and coughing, attempting to clear my airway and rid myself of the awful sensation.

My eyes are watering from the fit. I know I need to find some water, but I can't see clearly. When I'm finally able to open my eyes fully, between gasps for breath, I intend to look for said water, but inhale sharply at the scene before me instead.

Green smoke is seeping out of the cauldron at a rapid pace, already covering the ground with a murky layer. It's swirling around my ankles as it fills the room.

I desperately flip through the pages of my manual, looking for anything that can help me undo... whatever I did. Covering my mouth with my fist, I cough into it and frantically wave my arm in the air near the cauldron. I'm trying to dissipate some of the green smoke oozing into the room while my eyes rapidly skim potion names.

I'm panicking by the time the smoke reaches my knees with no sign of letting up. My lungs are screaming for air, and my eyes water, as the green fog becomes a thick wall, coating every surface in the room, with no pause in sight.

Abandoning my attempts to fix the problem I've created, I push through the green-tinged air blindly, searching for the wooden door nearby. I clutch my manual to my chest with my left hand, sliding my right along the wall.

Smiling in victory once my hand reaches the cool metal handle, I press down and open the door just enough for me to slip out, and quickly exit the room. Despite my hasty escape, the victorious feeling is short lived.

As I slam the door shut behind me, leaning against it to ensure it closes fully, I resume hacking up a lung. A puff of green smoke appears in the air by my face at the tail end of the coughing fit and my eyes widen in shock.

Did I swallow some of the smoke or is this going to become a permanent issue?

Testing my lungs, I huff out a few more breaths, thankful when the air appears to be clear. When I'm finally able to catch my breath, and rid myself of the fear of permanent green puff exhales, disappointment seeps deep into my bones.

I didn't realize this witch thing would be so hard. When my mom showed me our witching chamber a month ago, on my eighteenth birthday, I was filled with wonder and excitement. *I'm a witch! A real witch!* Played on repeat in my mind.

But little did I know, being a witch is actually super difficult.

Silly, naïve, newly eighteen-year old me, thought convincing the shifter council to let me go would be the biggest challenge I would face. Then, my grandmother appeared and determined it's a priority for me to earn my witching license as soon as possible. Since then, I've been plugging away, trying to channel a talent that is supposedly innate—brewing potions—but the more I try, the more I think maybe the witch gene skipped a generation. Now, wiser, eighteen years and one month old me is realizing: maybe I'm not cut out for this.

Interrupting my own morose thoughts, I shove off the door and head to the stone steps leading into my parent's room. I need to find my mom so she can help me clear out the chaos that I unintentionally caused.

I trudge upstairs, taking my time and holding the wall out of caution. Last week I slipped and tumbled down a fair portion of our secret passageway. It was a hard lesson in caution. Literally. The secret stone of my home is very unforgiving to land on.

After distractedly winding my way through the hall, I emerge into my parents' bedroom and replace the bookshelf. Wandering around the top floor, I quickly realize it's empty and jog downstairs, hoping my parents are in the kitchen.

I barrel through the doorway only to pull up short when I realize my parents and the Morts are sitting at the table in the kitchen nook and look to be having a deep, serious conversation.

Mr. Mort's eyes slide to me then back to my dad and he makes a huge, fake-sounding cough into his fist. Suddenly four pairs of eyes are on me and every face that was serious turns into a beaming smile.

I'm instantly suspicious.

"Are you here about Vlad? Is he back yet?" I demand, skipping pleasantries and delving right into the most important issue.

Tricia slides off the bench and comes to wrap me in a tight hug. "Mira, love. We haven't heard from Vlad yet, but I'm sure we will soon. This is typical of young wolves, to run for a while and blow off steam. There's no reason to worry..." The "Yet" is silent, but I hear the way her sentence lingers as if she left it off at the last second.

I return her squeeze tightly, then step back. "Okay, but will you have him call me as soon as you hear from him?" I ask. My words are more gentle than before, as I consider her tired eyes and messy ponytail.

"Of course, dear. Of course." She pats my shoulder consolingly before moving to slide back into the booth next to her husband. "Are you hungry? You came barreling down here like you were being chased by a rabid raccoon!"

I chuckle before memories of the green smoke sober me. Shuffling my feet, I mutter, "I actually need some help in the witching chamber."

My mom's smile dims immediately. "What is it this time?"

My hackles raise a little at her tone. Normally my parents don't get snippy with me, but I guess the fact that I've flooded the witching chamber, set three curtains on fire with some wayward liquid, and turned the neighbor's cat into a goldfish—all in the past week

—has everyone a bit on edge about my current witching abilities.

"I don't think it's TOO big of a deal," I start.

In response to my hedging, the adults immediately stand and briskly head for the entrance of the kitchen that leads to the stairs. I rush forward to catch up, shouting, "We might need some masks or something!"

A chorus of groans erupts down the hall in response.

<u>Click here to continue!</u>

REVIEWS

If you enjoyed this book, please consider leaving an honest review. Reviews truly are the lifeblood of any book and your opinion matters.

INTERESTED IN NEWS ABOUT BOOKS BY NICOLE MARSH?

Check out her socials here!

INTERESTED IN NEWS ABOUT BOOKS BY CASSY JAMES?

Check out her socials here!

BOOKS BY NICOLE MARSH

The Curse Trilogy (Paranormal Romance)

Cursed

Bound

Shattered

Standalone

The Con

BOOKS BY CASSY JAMES

The Curse Trilogy (Paranormal Romance)

Cursed

Bound

Shattered

Rockin' Love Duet

Electric Wounds

Intoxicating Hearts

Made in United States
Cleveland, OH
12 June 2025

17625283R10154